'**What can I do to make you take me seriously?**'

Will got up. 'Perhaps if I kissed you again— only differently this time?'

His mouth was very close to hers. Kate was conscious of a reckless kind of desire beating inside her. What harm was there in a kiss? He waited for a moment to give her time to draw away, and when she didn't his mouth came down to hers.

She opened her lips to his with a little sigh of pure desire.

Dear Reader

With the long summer evenings, what better way to relax than by reading a selection of stories which really take you away from it all? With four exciting contemporary romances, Mills & Boon will transport you to some of the most exotic locations in the world. Enjoy the luxury of those places you always wanted to visit...surely the perfect chance to dream of your ideal man! Look out for our summer packs in your local shops or contact our Reader Service and indulge yourself in the world of romance!

The Editor

Marjorie Lewty was born in Cheshire, and grew up between there and the Isle of Man. She moved to Liverpool and married there. Now widowed, she has a son, who is an artist, and a married daughter. She has always been drawn to writing and started with magazine short stories, then serials and finally book-length romances, which are the most satisfying of all. Her hobbies include knitting, music and lying in the garden thinking of plots!

Recent titles by the same author:

THE BEGINNING OF THE AFFAIR

LITTLE WHITE LIES

BY

MARJORIE LEWTY

MILLS & BOON LIMITED
ETON HOUSE,   18-24 PARADISE ROAD
RICHMOND,   SURREY   TW9 1SR

*First published in Great Britain 1993
by Mills & Boon Limited*

© Marjorie Lewty 1993

*Australian copyright 1993
Philippine copyright 1993
This edition 1993*

ISBN 0 263 78083 X

*Set in Times Roman 10 on 11 pt.
01-9307-58213 C*

Made and printed in Great Britain

CHAPTER ONE

FOR the third time in an hour the phone rang on the littered desk in Aunt Becky's office at the back of the small French hotel. Kate picked up the receiver gingerly, as if it might bite her. 'Hello?' She tried to sound businesslike, as a hotel receptionist might be expected to sound.

As she feared, she was met with a torrent of totally unintelligible French.

Groaning inwardly, she tried her best O-level effort. '*Je ne comprends pas. Parlez-vous Anglais?*'

No, of course whoever it was didn't speak English. They wouldn't, would they? After a few more frustrating moments, Kate gave it up. '*Pardonnez-moi,*' she croaked and replaced the receiver.

She sat back and ran a hand distractedly through her mane of auburn hair. Oh, lord, she might have lost a good booking for Becky. This was crazy; how was she going to cope? And why hadn't this man turned up— the man who was going to take over the management of the hotel while Becky was in hospital?

'He should be here soon,' Becky had whispered, as the nice French doctor helped her into his car to drive to the hospital in Rouen. 'He'll see to everything. So sorry, Kate, dear, so very sorry to spoil your holiday. So—so silly. . .' Then the pain had taken over and she hadn't been able to speak any more.

That was more than two hours ago. It was nearly six o'clock now and this wretched manager person hadn't put in an appearance.

The day had turned into an utter disaster. When she'd started out from London at the crack of dawn to catch the early morning ferry to Boulogne, Kate had been looking forward to a fortnight's holiday at Becky's little hotel in Normandy. A peaceful rest before she started to look for another job. Just what she needed.

Dear Becky—it had been so like her to know how Kate felt after Mother's funeral, and to come up with a practical solution. 'You need to get away for a real rest, love,' she'd said. 'You've had a bad time, coping with everything and keeping your job going as well. Haven't you got any holiday owing to you?'

Kate admitted that she had had to give up her job when Mother had needed attention twenty-four hours a day.

'Oh, you poor child; I didn't realise. No wonder you look washed out. Well, then, you must come over to me—the Ferme will be closed until Easter so we'll have the place to ourselves. Maria and Jacques will be away on holiday and I'm getting rid of the secretary-receptionist girl I've got at present—she's quite hopeless. We can do our own cooking and just laze about and if the weather is kind we can drive down to the beach. Normandy's often quite warm at this time of the year, and not really crowded. Now, do say you'll come.'

'I'd love to,' Kate had promised, and had added sadly, 'You're all the family I have left now.'

'You wouldn't... Forgive me, love, if I'm speaking out of turn—I was just wondering whether you'd thought of contacting your father again now. You haven't heard from him?'

'*No.*' Kate's mouth was tight, her face expressionless. 'I never want to see him again,' she said in a stony voice. 'Never. I hate him.'

Becky watched her compassionately. 'Dear Kate, I'm so sorry. I didn't realise you felt so badly about it still. Now, let's forget it and plan our holiday, shall we?'

That had been a fortnight ago, and this morning she had set out in her little red Metro with a sense of finding peace after the cares of the last weeks.

The trouble had soon begun. An accident on the motorway had meant long queues, and when she'd finally got to Dover she'd found that a strike of seamen on the French side of the Channel had meant shunting the sailings around so that she docked at Calais instead of Boulogne, which meant a longer drive on the French side.

Perhaps because she had been tired, and still shocked by what had happened, the drive through northern France had seemed longer than she remembered it, and she had got thoroughly confused trying to get through Rouen, where she had stopped to buy a present for her aunt. But Kate was a confident driver and naturally optimistic, and at last had arrived with relief at the small Normandy hotel—Ferme du Chemin Vert—which Becky had inherited from her elderly husband when he died five years ago.

Then had fallen the worst blow of all. Instead of welcoming her at the front door, as she usually did as soon as she heard the car, Becky had been hunched up, white-faced and in bad pain, on a sofa in the lounge.

'So ridiculous!' she lamented. 'I'm never ill, and then this morning...to be struck down...like this. I'm so *angry*.' She bit her lip hard.

Kate's anxious enquiries eventually put the situation in perspective. Becky's doctor, who was also an old friend of hers, had hurried round in response to a phone call, and insisted that Becky be taken to his own hospital in Rouen for tests and examination. It might be her appendix, or it might be something else, but whatever it was it needed immediate investigation. He would drive her to Rouen himself and, in fact, would be calling back for her any minute.

'He's such a nice man.' Becky managed her little crooked grin. 'I think he's a bit sweet on me. But Frenchmen can't make tea. Kate, darling, could you...?'

Hastily, Kate made a pot of tea and Becky sipped it thankfully, her teeth clattering against the cup. 'I tried to phone you not to come, but you must have already left. Your lovely holiday—all spoiled, and you needed it so badly,' she wailed.

'I could stay here and look after myself until you're better,' Kate suggested.

'That wouldn't do at all, love.' Becky, revived by the tea, sounded more like her old firm self. 'You see, I've been in touch with a friend of mine in the hotel business and he's promised to send me a man who can take over here until I get back. He's due to arrive this afternoon— name of Pierre Boudin. He's been on leave convalescing after a car crash, but he's OK now and he can look after the office work and see to the bookings and so on. The girl I've had in the office has been a complete disaster— she even managed to get the bookings mixed up. I'll have to find someone new when I get back.' Becky pushed back her short, wiry grey hair worriedly. 'I do hope this man's capable.'

Kate reached out and squeezed her hand. 'Don't you worry yourself, darling. I'll help him—we'll manage together.'

'Oh, but Katy, you can't possibly stay here—not alone in the hotel with a strange man. You don't know what——'

Kate grinned. 'I can cope with any man—strange or otherwise. And anyway, if he's recovering from a car crash I shouldn't think he'll have rape on his mind.'

Becky wasn't convinced. 'I won't hear of you...' she began agitatedly.

Kate said, 'Look, Becky, if it makes you feel happier I'll get myself a room for bed and breakfast at one of the hotels on the coast. I'm sure to get in somewhere at this time of year. Then I can pop in here and keep an eye on this Pierre Boudin person, and make sure he's doing his stuff.'

Becky sighed. 'You're sure you wouldn't rather go back to London?'

'Not on your nelly.' Kate grinned cheekily.

Becky smiled weakly. 'You're such a darling girl, my Kate,' she whispered and her eyes flooded with tears.

Down-to-earth, practical Becky weeping! Kate, who at the age of twenty-five had learned, the hard way, a certain toughness, was close to tears herself.

That had been two hours ago. Now it was nearly six o'clock and here she was, still alone, staring down at a desk which looked as if the incompetent secretary had been pushing papers about aimlessly on it. Kate glared at them, unable to decipher many words. She could almost have wished she'd elected to study modern languages in her last years at school instead of science and computer studies. Since her last visit Becky—always up to the minute—had installed a personal computer. It stood on a table in the corner, but it looked new and unused. The incompetent secretary had probably preferred to muddle about with pieces of paper.

Kate got up restlessly and stared through the window at the back garden, where Becky grew her own vegetables. Green sprouts were showing, but plenty of weeds too. Becky must have been feeling out of sorts for some time; it wasn't like her to tolerate weeds.

Beyond the garden a tree-lined lane wound its way out into the domesticated charm of the Normandy countryside, the lane that gave the hotel its name—Ferme du Chemin Vert. At least she could translate that, Kate thought wryly—Farm of the Green Lane. A lovely name, she'd always thought, and a dear little hotel, tucked away a few kilometres behind the coast. She remembered how she and Becky had enjoyed wandering along the lane in the evenings on her previous visits.

She had spent several holidays here in the past few years, in spite of Mother's silent disapproval.

Mother had never got on well with her elder sister, and when Kate had urged her to come along too she had drawn her lips tight. 'No, dear, Rebecca doesn't really want me. You go and enjoy yourself—she would much rather have you there.' And in spite of a lingering feeling of guilt, Kate had gone—and enjoyed herself. She loved her aunt, and admired the way she had managed her life and risen above difficulties. Kate sighed. It had been hard, sometimes, not to compare her with Mother, who had drawn into herself when trouble struck. But Becky's trouble could not compare with the agony that Mother had suffered. Becky had lost *her* husband through a peaceful death in advanced age. But Mother had been dealt the worst blow of all—had been deserted and left penniless.

Twelve years ago Becky, taking her annual trip touring her beloved French countryside, had come upon the inn. At first intrigued by its name, she had soon become even more intrigued by its handsome owner, an elderly widower called François, and he with her. To everyone's surprise Becky, who until then had referred to herself wryly as a 'spinster of uncertain age' had given up her good job in the Civil Service and married the man. Six happy, busy years had followed, and when François had died Becky had taken over the hotel and run it on her own. Helped by Marie and Jacques, who had worked at the hotel as long as they could remember, she had worked ceaselessly to make sure that the Ferme survived. And it *had* survived, and become prosperous, and had been well-reported in the lists of inns and small hotels.

It would be too bad if its reputation suffered because of this crisis. And it won't, if I have anything to do with it, Kate vowed fiercely.

Ah, at last! The sound of a car pulling up at the front! Kate ran down the passage, through the cosy lounge to

the entrance door, and looked eagerly across the grav-
elled frontage. It was a taxi, not a private car, which
had stopped at the gate. That figured, she thought. If
the manager person was recovering after an accident he
probably wouldn't be able to drive yet. All the more
reason why she should stay here, so that she and her
Metro would be at his disposal if he needed transport.

She watched him lever himself carefully out of the
front seat, leaning on a stick with one hand while the
other searched for coins to pay the driver.

He didn't look much like a hotel manager. Even allowing for the fact that in France professional men
seemed to dress less formally than in England, he was—
well—scruffy. He was tall and rangy, in worn jeans and
a faded blue shirt, with a red garment of some sort
knotted round his neck. His black hair was over-long
and lifted off his bony forehead in the evening breeze.
He looked rather like a a student, hiking round Europe
on a shoe-string, only he was too old to be a student.
In his thirties, probably.

The taxi drove away and he hitched his lumpy canvas
bag over his shoulder, picked up a small case, and stood
still, eyes moving over the hotel.

She hurried to meet him, rehearsing her first words.
'*Bonjour, monsieur. Je suis très heureuse que vous
avez arrivé.*'

Leaning on his stick, he turned his gaze briefly on to
her, one dark brow cocked. 'What a nice welcome,' he
drawled in perfect English.

Kate's generous mouth broke into a wide, beautiful
smile. 'Oh, you speak English. Thank goodness!' In her
relief she hadn't noticed the irony in his voice.

He shrugged. 'Why the surprise? It's supposed to be
a universal language.'

'Oh, I'm not surprised, I'm relieved,' she said, ignoring his patronising tone. 'You see, I've been trying
to cope here, but my French is very poor.'

He began to stump up towards the entrance door, leaning heavily on his stick. 'You're not Madame Arnot?' he said over his shoulder. 'No, of course you aren't. Where is she?'

'She's already left to go into hospital in Rouen. Didn't they tell you?'

He frowned. 'Why should they?'

'Well, I'd have thought...' Kate began, but already he'd reached the door and was limping into the lounge.

He was probably tired and even in pain. Kate decided she could allow for a little grumpiness. 'I'll show you your room,' she said kindly. 'You'd like to rest, I expect. It's on the ground floor—if you'll follow me.'

She led the way across the lounge, through the adjoining dining-room and along the passage beyond, and threw open the door of the small room at the end.

'We put you in here,' she said. 'Madame Arnot thought you might find the stairs a problem. The shower-room's through that door.'

He followed her in, dropping his canvas bag with a heavy thud. He was so tall that his dark head almost touched the ceiling.

He gave the room a cursory glance. 'I can't possibly manage in here,' he said curtly. 'It's much too small—and I need a table or a desk for my typewriter.'

Kate hung on to her patience. 'But you'll be using the office, surely?'

His head jerked round. 'Are you going to put the office at my disposal, then?'

'Why not? It seems the obvious thing.'

He passed a weary hand across his forehead. 'Nothing seems obvious at the moment. Oh, well, you'd better show me the office.'

He limped down the corridor after her to Becky's office with its littered desk. His eyes lit on the computer in the corner and he went over and examined it with the first show of interest he had displayed up to now.

'Is this part of the package?'' he said.

Kate stared. 'Sorry?'

He said resignedly, 'Am I allowed to use this while I'm here?'

'The computer? I don't see why not.'

He brightened a fraction. 'Oh, well, I suppose I could manage, if you haven't got a larger room prepared for me.'

Kate's patience was wearing very thin. 'That's big of you,' she said with a touch of acid in her normally pleasant voice.

He glanced at her as if she were part of the office furniture. 'I'm tired,' he said. 'Perhaps I could have some tea.'

Kate looked more carefully at his face and relented. He was very pale and there were shadows under his deep-set dark eyes. She noticed also how long his lashes were—black and glossy and curving almost on to his lean cheeks. He could be quite handsome if he didn't look so peevish.

'You wouldn't rather have coffee?' It seemed unusual for a Frenchman to demand tea.

'I said tea,' he told her curtly. 'I'll have it in my room.' His stick clattered on the tiles as he made his way back there.

Kate looked after him in exasperation. She would have liked to walk out and leave him to it, but he was quite obviously incapable of looking after himself at the moment. And for Becky's sake she'd have to make allowances—up to a point. But what a rude, uncouth boor! Even if he had been in hospital it was no excuse for his behaviour. She would have to make it clear to him that she wasn't going to put up with rudeness. Firming her lips, Kate went into the kitchen to put the kettle on.

The kitchen of the original farmhouse had been modernised and equipped for the running of the hotel. Kate always thought of it as a cheerful, bustling place, but now, without Marie in her striped apron, stirring something at the electric cooker, and Jacques pottering about outside in the yard polishing Becky's ancient black Renault, it felt empty and dismal. She switched on the light. They would be back soon, she told herself, and Becky, too, and everything would be normal again. A sudden chill struck Kate like a cold wind and she shivered. What if Becky didn't come back? What if the suspected appendix trouble turned out to be something really bad?

The kettle boiled and she thrust away the horrible thought. Not so soon after Mother—it would be too cruel. She mustn't be despondent; she must keep her energy to cope with the less-than-impressive temporary manager. She must try to forgive him for being so curt and demanding and put it down to the car crash that had laid him low. Very masculine men resented illness and took it out on all around, as she well knew from her experience in business.

She made tea and arranged it on a small tray with a plate of Marie's special cookies. Then she carried it along the corridor and tapped at the end door. There was a grunt from inside and she pushed open the door with her foot and peered into the room.

He was lying on the bed with his eyes closed. Kate walked across to the bed and stood looking down at him. He was long and lean and firmly muscled under the scruffy clothes. No spare flesh anywhere. With his eyes closed, the black lashes looked longer than ever. It wasn't fair that a man should have such gorgeous eyelashes. His mouth, in repose, was thin and long, his nose dominant, and his brow broad and slightly furrowed. His skin was a pale biscuit colour. He looked very French.

He opened his eyes and stared up at her. Meeting an intense black gaze, she felt a strong jolt inside. What was she doing, staring at the man like that? 'I've brought your tea,' she said rather coldly, putting the tray on the bedside table.

He levered himself up on the bed. 'Oh, thanks very much.' The first gracious words he'd spoken.

She hesitated by the door. 'What about dinner? I thought I'd fix some pasta for us. That OK for you?'

He stared, teapot in hand. 'You do the cooking?'

'Well, there's nobody else to do it,' she said and added, 'When you're feeling better you can look after yourself if you like. I take it you can cook?' A hotelier must presumably have worked his way up through the kitchen.

He shook his head slowly. 'This is certainly a curious kind of hotel. Yes, I like pasta. Plenty of tomato sauce.'

'Right,' she said. 'About half-past seven.' She went out and closed the door.

Back in the kitchen she found that Becky had evidently stocked up for the holiday. There was a selection of pasta in the store cupboard. In the fridge she found tomatoes, olive oil, onions, fruit, cheese—everything to make an acceptable meal. Perhaps his high and mightiness would unbend when he had fed, she thought, attacking onions rather savagely with a cook's knife.

The phone rang in the office and she swore softly as she hurried to answer it. If it was someone speaking French she'd jolly well go and stir up the comatose temporary manager, tired or not. She was tired too, she thought crossly, picking up the phone.

'Hello, is that you, Katherine?' said a light masculine voice, and Kate's heart sank. It was a relief that it wasn't someone speaking French, but on the other hand she didn't particularly want to talk to Edward, who was inclined to fuss.

'Hello, Edward,' she said, rather tonelessly.

'My dear—are you all right? You sound very tired.' The precise solicitor's voice reached her rather faintly. It was probably coming from somewhere in Yorkshire, where he was visiting his mother.

'I'm OK, Edward,' she said. 'It's been a long day, that's all.'

Edward clucked his tongue. 'I knew I shouldn't have let you drive all that way alone.'

Kate sighed. 'I'm all right, Edward. I'm fine.'

'Oh, well, that's OK, then. How did you find your aunt?'

Kate swallowed. 'Her usual cheerful self.' That was a long way from the truth, but it couldn't be helped. She changed the subject. 'Did you have a good run and is your mother well?'

Edward hadn't wanted her to come to Normandy. He had wanted her to go to Harrogate with him to meet his mother, but she had balked at that. It had seemed too much like making a decision and she wasn't ready for that. One of the things she had been planning for this holiday was to spend time thinking hard about herself and Edward. She knew he was leading up to a proposal of marriage—Edward would never propose anything less conventional. She was sure he was a good, kind man who would make an excellent husband. Such qualities as that were supremely important to Kate and she thought that some time she might marry him. But certainly not yet.

He enquired about her journey and she told him a little about the drive, but nothing about what had met her at the end of it. Edward would insist on her leaving if he knew she was here alone with a strange man. Edward had no right to caution or advise her. She supposed she should take it as a compliment that he always seemed to want to. It annoyed her that she should feel a little guilty about deceiving him. Truthfulness was something that Kate felt very strongly about.

'Mother is very disappointed that you didn't come with me,' Edward said. 'She was looking forward to meeting you.' A pause. 'It's pretty cold in these parts—you may be having the best of the weather.'

They discussed the weather for a few more minutes, then Edward said, 'I'll only be staying about a week or so. I'll ring you again when I get back to London.'

'Yes, you do that,' Kate said brightly. 'Give my regards to your mother.'

'I will, Katherine.' There was a pause and she thought he had hung up. Then he said, 'I—I miss you, you know.'

'Thank you, Edward, that's very nice.' She wasn't going to tell another lie and say she was missing him too.

'Oh, by the way,' he went on hurriedly, 'I've posted a letter to you. You should get it tomorrow or the next day.'

'Thank you,' Kate said again, wondering what Edward could possibly have to say to her in a letter that he couldn't say on the phone.

They said goodbye and she went back to chopping the onions, thinking rather vaguely about Edward, who seemed to be in another world at the moment.

She hadn't known Edward very long. Mr Truslove, the senior partner in the firm of solicitors which had looked after Mother's interests at the time of the divorce ten years ago, had retired about the time of Mother's death and Edward had taken his place, attending to probate of the will and other matters concerned with Mother's estate. At first Kate couldn't understand why it should be taking so long. Mother couldn't have left much money behind her, poor darling. But after a short time it became clear that Edward's interest in her was more than professional. Phone calls and little dinners to discuss certain aspects of the will had led to invitations to the cinema, once to a concert.

Kate, shocked by her mother's sudden death, had allowed herself to drift into being taken for granted by Edward—until she was brought up short when Edward took it for granted that she should want to spend her holiday with him at his mother's home in Yorkshire. Then she had told him very definitely that she had promised to visit her aunt in Normandy. A certain coolness on Edward's part hadn't made her change her mind and finally he had accepted the situation.

But he hadn't yet forgiven her—she could sense his huffiness from the phone conversation. Oh, well, she couldn't worry about Edward now. She had more important things on her mind, the principal one being that she had to find out how to get along with this impossible temporary manager.

She had a feeling that it wasn't going to be easy.

CHAPTER TWO

THE next thing to do was to find herself a room in the hotel for the night. Kate hadn't asked Becky which room had been prepared for her, because she wasn't supposed to be staying here.

She smiled ruefully now as she explored the six bedrooms upstairs, each with bath. Of course she had to stay. A fat lot of use Monsieur Pierre Boudin would be on his own. Demanding and arrogant, he expected to be waited on hand and foot. Either Becky's hotelier friend hadn't explained the circumstances to him, or he was just naturally a chauvinist pig. A man who used any woman around to pander to his needs. With those fantastic eyes he probably never had to look very hard. He was the type of man whom Kate distrusted and disliked.

So far as she could see, none of the rooms was ready for use. Probably Becky had been taken ill this morning before she'd had a chance to make up a bed. Kate chose the room at the top of the stairs, whose window overlooked a large cherry tree, and busied herself stocking up from the linen cupboard on the landing. She carried her travel bag up from the office and unpacked neatly. After all the hassle of the day she felt dusty and bedraggled and her hair was a mess.

She took a shower and washed her hair, drying it quickly with the small travelling drier she had brought with her. Then she stood in front of the wardrobe and surveyed her clothes. Suddenly it occurred to her that she had never explained to the Boudin man exactly who she was. That might account for his peculiar behaviour. He had probably taken her for a hotel servant who had

19

come over from England for the season. She would have to disabuse his mind of that idea very firmly.

She slipped on the most expensive dress she had brought with her—a silk jersey in a shade of green which almost matched her eyes and did wonders for the fine, faultless skin that she always thought was her best point. Then she plaited her glossy dark red hair and arranged it into a stylish knot on the top of her head. A faint dusting of eyeshadow, a touch of lipgloss, small drop earrings of mother-of-pearl, and she was ready.

Surveying her reflection in the looking-glass in the door of the heavy antique wardrobe, she decided that it was marvellous what clothes did for your confidence. She felt a new girl and ready to deal with any male chauvinists around—meaning Monsieur Boudin. However much she deplored his attitude she had to get on the right side of him, for Becky's sake.

Downstairs in the kitchen she found one of Marie's voluminous aprons and tied it round her slim middle, pulled up her sleeves, and set to work.

Half an hour later, all was ready. On the kitchen table, covered with a cheerful red and white checked cloth, reposed a dish of salad, a baguette, yellow local butter and a platter of Camembert cheese. Two wine glasses glittered in the bright ceiling-light and a bottle of Becky's special Calvados stood beside them waiting to be opened. A delicious aroma rose from the big pan on the stove.

There—he couldn't fault that, surely?

Kate went along the passage and tapped smartly on the door. 'Dinner's ready,' she called out loudly. 'In the kitchen, along the passage.'

The sound of something being dropped inside the room, followed by a muttered curse, told her he was awake. She chuckled as she made her way back to the kitchen. The back bedroom *was* rather small for a big man, especially a big man handicapped by a gammy leg. She hoped he wouldn't smash up the furniture. All

Becky's rooms were furnished with heavy antiques, so probably they would be safe.

She heard him stumping along the corridor and smiled pleasantly. 'In here—all ready for you.'

When he came in he looked at the table, not at Kate. 'We dine in the kitchen, do we? Primitive stuff!'

Kate turned her back and went across to the stove as he lowered himself clumsily into a chair. 'What did you expect?' she enquired, carefully keeping her voice amused. 'Service à la Ritz?' She spooned pasta on to two plates and carried them to the table. 'Will you open the bottle?'

He picked up the bottle and studied the label. 'Calvados? Strong stuff—oh, well, I need that.' He opened the bottle expertly while Kate stood beside the table watching. How strong his hands were—good hands with slim brown fingers and a fine powdering of dark hair. Sensitive hands. Not like the man himself; he was anything but sensitive. He was boorish—why, he hadn't even bothered to brush his hair and his chin was prickly with a dark growth of hair.

He put down the bottle and for the first time since he had entered the kitchen he looked up at her as she whipped off Marie's big overall.

'Well, well!' he breathed. His eyes widened and his gaze passed slowly, insolently over her from the carefully arranged topknot of shining dark red hair, over the green jersey dress which clung softly to her small breasts, to her long legs, neat, slim ankles and black kid pumps. Kate could feel the heat gathering in her cheeks as the silence lengthened.

'Why *all* the glamour?' he drawled. 'If it's intended for my benefit I may as well tell you, my girl, that you've got the wrong idea.'

Her breath caught in her throat. 'W-what are you trying to say?'

His mouth curled into a sneer. 'That I don't require servicing at the moment.'

'Oh, you—you...' she choked. Her hand went out automatically and delivered a smart smack across his cheek.

Maddeningly, he laughed aloud. Then, before she knew what was happening, he had encircled her waist and pulled her down across his knees.

'You need a lesson, my girl,' he ground out between his teeth. She struggled and kicked and turned her head away, but he grasped her chin with one hand and forced it towards him as his mouth came down on hers. His kiss was hard and punishing and Kate felt a wild answering rush of anger running through her like strong brandy. Her body twisted this way and that, writhing helplessly in his grasp. Then, as she felt his tongue invade her mouth, she used the only weapon she had left, she bit as hard as she could.

He released her immediately and she flopped on to the floor. 'You little she-cat,' he muttered, dabbing at his mouth with one of Becky's snowy table-napkins.

Kate struggled to her feet and pulled down her dress. The plait of hair was hanging down her back and she pinned it up with trembling fingers as she sank limply into her chair, breathing fast.

'I'm wounded,' he moaned, inspecting the napkin.

'Pooh! One drop of blood—I should have done better than that.'

He looked across the table and for the first time he seemed actually to see her. 'Do you make a habit of cannibalising your lovers, then?'

She met the black, liquid eyes bravely. 'I don't,' she said, 'make a habit of having lovers.'

'Really? I find that difficult to believe. Red hair—green eyes—luscious mouth—a potent brew!'

Kate threw back her head and regarded him down her straight little nose. 'And I find you insulting and boorish, *monsieur*,' she retorted icily.

She saw a gleam of amusement in the fantastic dark eyes and realised with a shock that in a crazy way she was rather enjoying this confrontation.

'And I——' she began.

Then the wall-phone buzzed behind the table. Kate waited for a moment, to see if the new manager would start to do his job and answer it. When he ignored it completely she picked up the receiver herself. As she had feared, a stream of French greeted her. Well, she wasn't going to try to cope with this; why should she?

She held the receiver out to him across the table. 'Go on,' she said. 'Answer it; I can't understand a word.'

For a moment she thought he was going to refuse. Then he gave her a long, hard look and took the receiver from her. '*Allo... Oui... Oui...bon...*' He pulled a notebook from the pocket of his jeans and began to jot down words. Kate could hear a voice clacking away at the other end of the line. Let him deal with it all, she thought wearily. I've had enough.

It was quite a short message. He handed the receiver back to Kate and she replaced it. 'Anything urgent?' she enquired.

He said, 'I suppose it makes sense to you. It was someone called Raymond. The gist of it was that he was very sorry but the man he was going to send——' he looked down at the notebook '—name of Pierre Boudin, has had a relapse and won't be able to come for at least another week. He was very apologetic and hoped it wouldn't be an inconvenience et cetera, et cetera.'

Kate sank back limply, staring at the man opposite, trying to take it in.

At last she whispered through dry lips. 'I thought... Then you're not Pierre Boudin?'

'Of course I'm not,' he snapped. 'Now, do you mind telling me——?'

'Then if you aren't Pierre Boudin, who are you and why are you here?' Kate said.

He took a long, deep breath. 'Let's just end this charade, shall we? My name's Raven—Will Raven. I booked in to this hotel a few days ago for a fortnight's stay. I was recommended that it was a quiet, friendly place where I'd be well looked after. I arrive to be greeted by an employee who speaks no French, to be given a room the size of a postage stamp, to be expected to use the office if I want to do my private work, to be served a meal in the kitchen and warned that I shall have to do my own cooking. And then to be given a definite come-on by a . . .' He paused suddenly, eyes narrowing. 'Who are you, anyway? What are you?'

Kate's brain was working overtime, if chaotically. 'Look,' she said, 'there's been a complete misunderstanding all round. First of all, the hotel is closed to visitors until Easter. Second, I'm not an employee; I'm Madame Arnot's niece, and I, too, have come for a quiet holiday. Third, there was definitely no come-on, except in your typically conceited masculine imagination.' She paused for breath. 'I don't know about you, but I'm hungry. I've driven from London today and haven't eaten properly since breakfast. Suppose we finish our meal, take our coffee into the lounge, and straighten things out then?'

He'd been watching her with increasing surprise, and now he said, 'You're Madame Arnot's niece, did you say? It might be easier if I knew your name.'

'I'm Katherine Lovell,' she said.

He lay back in his chair, eyes narrowed.

'Is there anything odd about that?' She picked up her fork and attacked the pasta.

'Odd? No, of course not,' he said smoothly. 'Except that the whole business is rather odd, don't you think?

But yes, I agree that it would be sensible to eat. I've been living on hospital food for the last ten days and I admit the pasta looks tempting.' He pulled a wry face, putting the napkin up to his mouth again. 'That is, of course, if I find it possible to eat, having been mortally wounded.' The dark eyes that met her surprised ones were dancing with amusement.

Kate felt a hot flush rising into her cheeks. She couldn't remember blushing before—ever. 'Shall we forget that little episode?' she said.

'You may, if you can,' he said enigmatically. 'I may not find it so easy.' He attacked the pasta with enthusiasm, leaving Kate at a loss for words, and neither of them spoke again until the pan was empty.

It was a day full of surprises. Certainly Kate would never have dreamed that half an hour later she would be sitting before a crackling log fire in the comfort of the lounge, drinking coffee in perfect amity with Will Raven.

She had explained all. They had even searched the books in the office together.

'You say you booked in for March the fourteenth?' Kate said. 'Just for one—you didn't book in your wife as well?'

'I don't have a wife,' he said with a sideways glance at her as they bent over the bookings record.

'Oh,' was all that Kate found to reply to that. Hastily she ran her finger down the page. 'Here we are. William Raven. March the fourteenth. Single room with bath for fourteen days. And today's March the fourteenth. The wretched secretary must have forgotten that the hotel would be closed.'

Kate slammed the book down in exasperation. 'My aunt was getting rid of her because of incompetence. She certainly went out on a high note. I'm terribly sorry about it.'

They went back to the lounge and settled down in front of the fire and Will Raven moaned about his enforced stay in hospital with a fractured ankle. 'Such a stupid thing to happen—I was damn careless.'

'You mustn't blame yourself,' Kate soothed. She was feeling pleasantly relaxed, lying back in a big easy-chair. 'These things can happen to anyone, any day.'

'Really?' He looked lazily at her from his chair on the opposite side of the wide brick hearth.

'Well—everyone seems to drive so fast in France.'

'Who said anything about driving? It wasn't driving that accounted for this.' He indicated his leg.

'Oh,' she said blankly. 'I thought... Of course, I was still mixing you up with Pierre Boudin. I was told he'd been in a car crash.'

'Oh, my little mishap wasn't even as dramatic as a car crash. Actually I had a slight altercation with a spider.'

'A what?' Kate squeaked.

'A black one with short legs and a big hairy body. It was poised on the ceiling above my bed one night.' He shuddered. 'I'm allergic to spiders; they terrify the day-lights out of me.'

'Oh, dear!' Kate refrained from laughing. It was no joke to be afraid of spiders—actually she rather liked him for admitting it. It made him seem very human. 'What did you do?'

'Like a blithering fool I climbed on the dressing-table and flicked it off. It fell on the bed—ugh—and I fell on the floor. End of story.'

'Oh, poor you!' Kate sympathised. 'I know how you must have felt. I've got a thing about beetles myself.'

He laughed. He had a nice laugh, deep and throaty. 'We mustn't set up in farming together, then. We'll have to think of something else.'

It was a joke, of course. But as he met her eyes across the space between them the word 'together' seemed quite natural, as if they were really planning a shared future.

Pull yourself together, Kate, you've only known the man a couple of hours. She put down her coffee-cup and said, 'I suppose we must be practical. What will you do?'

'Do? I don't feel like doing anything just now. I'm very comfortable where I am.'

'I mean, where will you go? You'll have to find another hotel; you can't stay here.'

'Why not?'

Kate felt suddenly flustered. She fluttered her hands. 'For one thing the hotel's closed until Easter; it's not geared up to cope with visitors.'

'And the other thing?' He was looking at her closely, dark brows raised.

'Well—I'd have thought it was obvious. I'm here on my own at present. I wouldn't——'

'You wouldn't trust me, after my exhibition in the kitchen? Even if I promised to—er—respect your wishes?'

Kate felt the heat rising into her cheeks, remembering how it had felt to lie across his knees and be pressed close against his lean, hard body. It had been a new experience. No man had ever got close enough to her to manhandle her like that. Edward's goodnight kisses were pleasant, controlled, but then Edward was a very controlled person. There was no—no *danger* in kissing Edward. No challenge, no excitement. Nothing that she had felt, for a wanton moment, in Will Raven's arms.

She said as coolly as she could, 'How would I know whether to trust you or not? You're a stranger.' But even as she said the words she thought in amazement, He isn't a stranger, though; I feel as if I've known him for years.

This was ridiculous; it must stop immediately, and there was one good way to stop it. 'Anyway,' she went on, 'I'm engaged—well, nearly.'

He hadn't taken his eyes from her face. 'And your nearly fiancé would not approve, of course.'

'Edward would have a fit,' she said firmly.

He nodded in a resigned kind of way. 'Well, I suppose we wouldn't want that to happen. I shall have to remove myself from the premises forthwith. Do you want me to go tonight? And have you any suggestions as to where? I don't feel quite up to trekking round the countryside on foot at the moment. I suppose I could get a taxi from somewhere—it's a darned nuisance that I can't drive,' he added with an utterly unconvincing sigh of regret.

Kate wouldn't allow herself to be manipulated by such a blatant appeal to her better nature. 'I'll look in the telephone directory,' she said firmly, getting to her feet, hoping she could solve the mysteries of a French directory. Were there 'yellow pages' in this country? she wondered.

He said, 'I'd like very much to stay, you know. I wouldn't be any trouble. I could look after my own food and I think I'd be useful to you until you get some more help. With your language difficulty, I mean.'

She stood looking down at him uncertainly. 'Why do you want to stay? You'd be much more comfortable in another hotel.'

'Possibly. But I'd be quiet here. And I must admit that I'd really like to have the use of that computer in the office. You see, I've got a deadline on a book I'm writing and this little hospital effort has set me back. A word processor—it looks similar to the one I'm used to—would be a godsend.'

It sounded convincing enough. And it *would* be a relief to have someone around who spoke the language. She hesitated. 'Well—I suppose——'

'That's wonderful,' he said immediately, smiling widely. 'I promise you won't regret it. I'll behave myself impeccably. I wouldn't dream of trying it on with any girl who's in love with another chap.'

Hearing it put into words gave Kate quite a shock. *Was* she in love with Edward? That was a question she would have to face on this holiday. Possibly the proximity of an attractive man might make it easier to decide.

She gave her shoulders a little shake. She was in no condition to think about things like that tonight. There were more serious matters to consider.

She glanced at her watch. Becky's doctor had given her the number of the hospital and told her to wait until later this evening to make enquiries. Now that the moment had come she felt a sinking feeling in the pit of her stomach. Suddenly she was very glad she wasn't alone to cope with the telephone.

She said, 'If you're going to stay—for tonight at least—will you do something to help me straight away, now?'

'Anything,' said Will Raven fervently.

'Speak to the hospital for me and try to find out how my aunt is. I'm worried about her.'

'Of course,' he said, getting up immediately. 'Let's go.'

Kate had left a note of the phone number in the office. Will looked at the name of the hospital in Rouen. 'I know it,' he said. 'It's an excellent place; your aunt should get top treatment.' He dialled the number and, as he went through the business of discovering the right person to speak to, Kate listened to the rapid flow of words coming along the line and felt more and more thankful that he was there. She would never have coped with this herself, using her halting French. And she had to admit, also, that it was comforting not to be alone, in case the news was bad. 'Oh, please—please—let her be all right.'

He replaced the receiver at last and Kate looked up into his face questioningly, her nails digging into her palms.

'Not very much definite,' he told her. 'Your aunt is sleeping at present; they have given her a sedative for the pain. She has been examined and it seems likely that they will carry out an exploratory operation tomorrow morning. More than that they wouldn't say.'

'Then it isn't just a straightforward appendix?' Kate said in a small voice. 'That seemed likely.'

He shook his head. 'I shouldn't think so from what the sister said.' His eyes rested on Kate's white face. 'I couldn't be sure, of course, but I got the impression that they weren't unduly worried about her—so *you* mustn't worry,' he added gently.

She sank into a chair weakly and blinked up at him, her eyes swimming. 'I'll try not to. Aunt Becky's very dear to me—she's the only family I have left now.'

'Your parents?' he questioned.

'My mother died just over a month ago.'

'And your father?'

She looked away from him, through the dark window, and the tears dried in her eyes. The light from the office fell across the garden and lit up the thick swirling mist that was coming down. The dried-up stumps of Brussels sprouts which hadn't been removed since the winter stood up like grey ghosts. Uprooted pea haulm waited in a heap to be removed. All dead; all finished.

Kate's mouth was a grin line. 'I have no father,' she said stonily.

She didn't notice the look of compassion that crossed the man's face. He held out his hand. 'Come on, let's go back and see if there's any coffee left,' he said, and she let him lead her back to the fire.

The coffee-jug was empty. 'I'll go and make some more,' Kate said wearily. She could take a good deal of pressure normally, but the events of the day were finally taking their toll.

Will Raven pushed her gently into her chair. 'You're all in,' he said. 'I'll make the coffee. If you're going to let me stay I must do my share of the chores.'

'I don't . . .' Kate began, but he had picked up his stick and limped towards the kitchen.

She relaxed into the comfort of the easy-chair. Who'd have thought anyone could change so quickly? No hint remained of the arrogant chauvinist pig he had been at first. If he was going to be so pleasant and helpful then she was glad she had agreed to let him stay. And it would be invaluable to have someone who spoke French.

She yawned. Admit it, Kate, you're glad he's staying, never mind thinking up reasons. She closed her eyes and the warmth from the fire played on her cheeks. She was sure Becky would understand, if she could explain it all to her. Becky—dear Becky—she'd be all right; she *must* be all right. She yawned again. Oh, she was so *tired*; she hovered between sleeping and waking.

She opened her eyes to see Will standing with his back to the fire, gazing down at her. There was something in his stillness, in the way the long-lashed eyes were fixed on her face, that suggested that he might have been standing there for some time.

Kate sat up with a jerk. 'Oh, I—I was almost asleep, I think.'

He moved then, smiled. 'Not surprising. You must have had a long day, driving from London. You work there?' He sat down and poured out coffee from the fresh supply he must have brought with him. 'What do you do?'

'At the moment I go around training people who buy computers from the firm I work for.'

'A lady boffin?' He grinned at her.

Kate smiled back. 'I suppose so. This coffee's very good.'

'One of my minor accomplishments. It goes with the writing job.'

'What do you write?'

'Anything that sells. At the moment I'm doing a mystery-thriller. I'd just reached the bit where the detective tells his sidekick that he knows who did the murder, when I fell off the dressing-table.'

'Very frustrating for you,' Kate said solemnly.

He pushed a log back on to the fire and watched the sparks fly up the chimney. 'I'm glad you're going to let me stay,' he said.

'And have the use of Becky's computer?' Kate reminded him.

'Of course, that's a bonus. With a lady boffin all laid on to put me right if I get in a muddle. Will you charge a fee, or do it for love?' In the firelight she could see little devils dancing lazily in his eyes.

'I won't do it at all if you're going to be provocative,' Kate said severely. She stood up. There was a certain danger in this light-hearted exchange—almost a touch of intimacy. 'I'm off to bed now; I can't keep awake any longer. Can you manage in that small room, do you think?'

'I'll manage in a dog kennel so long as you don't turn me out. I don't feel like sleep just now, I think I'll stay by the fire for a while.'

Kate nodded. 'Thank you for handling the phone calls for me.' She paused. 'You know, I took you for a Frenchman—that was part of the misunderstanding. You—sort of—look French to me, and you speak the language so fluently.'

'Not surprising,' he said. 'My mother was French. I've lived a good deal of my life in Paris.'

'I see. She's—not still alive?'

'She died nearly eight years ago. She was a lovely, kind lady. I still miss her a lot.'

'And your father?'

'I didn't know him at all. He died soon after I was born. Poor Mama had to cope with me on her own,' he added wryly. 'I must have been a sore trial to her.'

Kate tried to think of something to say, but nothing came. After a pause she said, 'Well, I'll really go or I'll be asleep on my feet. You'll put out all the lights?'

'Trust me,' he said.

She nodded. It was very strange, but somehow she felt she *could* trust him, and not merely to put out the lights.

'Goodnight, Will,' she said, turning to the door.

He smiled his lazy, charming smile at her. 'Goodnight, Kathy,' he said.

She stopped as if he had struck her, spun around like a whirlwind. 'Don't you call me that,' she shot at him. 'Don't ever call me that again.'

Will was on his feet in an instant. 'I'm sorry,' he said. 'I thought——'

'Well, don't think,' she snapped. She could feel hot tears smarting behind her eyes. 'Just—don't do it.'

She turned and fled upstairs, leaving him staring after her in amazement.

CHAPTER THREE

KATE closed the bedroom door and leaned her back against it, breathing fast, her eyes closed. Oh, why did Will have to say that, and in that tone, just as *he* used to say it all those years ago? 'Goodnight, Kathy,' he would say fondly, looking up from his evening paper. 'Sleep tight, little kitten.'

Kathy. Nobody else had ever called her Kathy. Such a small thing to pierce, for a moment, through the thick layer of ice she'd built round the memory of misery and betrayal. But only for a moment, she assured herself, as she began to get ready for bed. The ice would soon form again over the memory of herself at fifteen, the girl who had nearly had her heart broken when her adored father had walked out and left her and her mother penniless, ten years ago.

But she shouldn't have turned on Will Raven like that; it wasn't his fault. It was important that she didn't antagonise him—for the sake of Becky and the hotel. Because, truth to tell, she didn't know how she was going to get through the next week or so without him. Tomorrow she would apologise, make some explanation—hint that it had reminded her of a broken romance or something. She'd have to lie to him and she hated lying, but it couldn't be helped.

She smiled as she got ready for bed, thinking of Will Raven. He had certainly changed his tune when he found out who she was. It was really quite amusing the way he had mistaken her for a girl on the make—a tart, to put it crudely. His response had been crude too. Kate had never been kissed like that before, so brutally; she had never allowed a man to get close enough. Passionate lovemaking wasn't her style—which was one of the reasons she'd allowed herself to drift into a kind of understanding with Edward. Edward had kissed her goodnight—twice—but there had been no loss of control, no threat in Edward's kisses.

Will Raven's kiss had been quite a different matter. There'd been plenty of threat in that. She was glad she'd shown him that she wasn't prepared to take any nonsense of that kind from him. Of course, he hadn't known who she was when he'd put on his macho act, and there had been a kind of primitive satisfaction in getting her own back. Too primitive, she decided wryly. She hadn't known she could behave with such ferocity; for a moment she'd felt quite abandoned. Oh, well, it wouldn't happen again, she assured herself, snuggling down under the fleecy duvet.

Ten minutes later she was fast asleep and a little smile still lingered round her mouth.

Kate slept soundly and wakened early. She had opened her window last night, a luxury she could never allow herself in London, and the fresh spring air was blowing in from the fields this morning, bringing with it the smell of earth and growing things. Her head was clear and she remembered in a flash all that had happened yesterday.

Showering and dressing quickly in jeans and a white woollen shirt, she worried about Becky. But there was nothing she could do for her at the moment and the sensible thing was to keep the flag flying for her at the hotel. Which undoubtedly meant keeping on the right side of Will Raven.

Before she reached the bottom of the stairs she smelt coffee, and in the kitchen she found Will himself, sitting at the table, looking smug and drinking from a red coffee beaker. He looked rather more presentable this morning. He was still wearing the same shirt and jeans, but he had shaved and brushed his hair. He looked almost handsome, if you liked that kind of dark good looks, Kate thought.

'Good morning, Kate,' he said cheerfully, waving towards the espresso machine, 'I thought I'd try to atone for making you angry last night. May I give you a mug of my special brew?'

'Oh. Oh, thanks.' Somewhat taken aback, Kate sat down while the machine hissed and spluttered. The thought occurred that if it had been Edward he would have taken umbrage at the unreasonable way she'd attacked him last night.

Will placed a tiny mug of very black coffee before her and she smiled her thanks. 'Lovely—just what I needed. I've always been scared to use that machine—you must show me how it works.'

He raised dark eyebrows. 'What an admission from a lady boffin! I'd have thought all technology was an open book to you.'

'You just wait until you can't work Aunt Becky's word processor,' she came back at him.

Things were going well, she decided with relief. A friendly atmosphere was being established between them. She said, 'You've taken the wind out of my sails. I was going to apologise to you for losing my temper last night. It was just that—you touched me on a raw spot.'

He smiled knowingly. 'I take it there was a man involved?'

'Of course,' she admitted. That was true at any rate.

He nodded. 'You have my sympathy. One needs time to get over it. Now, how do you like your eggs? Five minutes?'

Kate jumped to her feet. 'You must let me wait on you. You're a visitor to this hotel, remember. And you're an invalid.'

'Almost better,' he told her with satisfaction, taking a few steps towards her, arms outstretched, pretending to balance shakily. 'Look, no hands!'

Kate's eyes widened. He was very close to her, and for a crazy moment she thought he meant to put his arms round her. She felt an odd quiver inside as she drew back. Then she laughed aloud. 'You *are* an idiot, Will Raven.'

He dropped his arms. 'That's what I like to hear. I knew I could make you laugh if I tried hard enough.'

'Oh, dear,' she said, 'have I been such a grouch?'

He shook his head and suddenly he was serious. He said slowly, 'No, but you're worried, aren't you? About your aunt and about being stuck with this hotel on your hands, and everything?'

'Yes,' said Kate slowly. 'I am. You're very perceptive.'

'I mean to help,' he said simply.

She said, 'Life in the great big world has taught me that everyone has a motive for what they do. What's yours?'

He pulled a face at her. 'You're a hard woman, that you are, Miss Lovell. But remember, I write mysteries. I like to keep the big surprise until the end.'

She sighed. 'OK, then I accept with gratitude. Now, let's get on with breakfast—I'm starving. And you sit down—*I'll* boil the eggs and make the toast.'

Breakfast was a companionable affair. They discussed computers, and Will gave her a run-down of the plot of his book, as far as it went.

Kate was intrigued. 'You must tell me the end if you leave before you finish it. *I* think it was the chauffeur who did the murder.'

'Ah,' he said darkly, 'you do, do you? That's interesting.'

'*Was* it the chauffeur?'

The dark eyes danced, meeting hers. 'Wouldn't you like to know?'

Kate sighed. 'OK, let's get you going on Becky's word processor, then. The sooner you finish the book the sooner I'll be proved right.'

An hour later, in the office, Will sat back and ran a hand through his crisp dark hair. 'Thank the lord for lady boffins,' he said with feeling. 'This software's different from my system; I'd have been going up the wall by now without you, Kate. I think I've got the hang now, though. I'm in your debt.'

Kate was standing behind his chair, leaning over his shoulder to point out the command for altering a margin. As he touched the keys at her instruction she moved back a little and her eyes seemed to focus themselves on the place where the hair curled in at the back of his neck. There was something boyish and rather endearing about his neck and she had an insane urge to lean down and press her lips against it. She jerked up, her heart racing, and at the same moment he turned his head round towards her.

'Got it!' he exclaimed triumphantly. 'Why, what's the matter, Kate? Are you OK?'

She blinked dazedly. 'Yes, I just felt—yes, of course I'm OK.' It couldn't be, could it—you couldn't fall in love like that all in a split second, with someone you'd only known a few hours? No, of course you couldn't. It was just a physical reaction to an attractive man. It might happen any time, she told herself. She'd been taken by surprise because it had never happened to her like that before. She slid into a chair, passing a hand across her forehead. 'I don't know what——'

'I do,' Will said promptly. 'You're worried stiff about your aunt. Should we ring the hospital to enquire, do you think? I'll do whatever you say.'

She grasped the excuse. 'Oh, would you? Thank you so much.'

She sat watching him as he put the call through. How strong his face was! In spite of the light-hearted chit-chat that came so easily to him, you could sense the underlying sensitivity in the wide brow, in the thinnish, sculptured line of his mouth, in the firmness of his chin.

Suddenly Kate was overcome with guilt. Here she was getting all worked up over a man when Becky was—was perhaps lying supine on an operating table somewhere. She shook her shoulders as if she could shake off the madness that had so surprised her.

Will replaced the receiver. 'Not easy to get information out of them. But I gathered that Madame Arnot has had her operation and is back in the ward. More than that I couldn't find out.' He leaned across and covered her hands with his. 'She'll be all right, Kate; I'm sure she will. I'll ring up again after lunch.'

But as it turned out that wasn't necessary, for, soon after lunch, as Kate was starting to wash up the dishes and Will had returned to his word processor, Becky's doctor friend wandered into the kitchen.

'I invite myself in.' He beamed jovially. 'I am at 'ome here, *non*? How are you, *mademoiselle*? I bring you news of *madame*.' He was smiling, so the news must be good, Kate thought with relief.

She had met the doctor briefly yesterday afternoon, when he had called to drive Becky to the hospital. He was a poppet, she had decided, a smallish, plump, middle-aged man with twinkling dark eyes and a neat little beard.

'Oh, please tell me—how is she?' Kate sat him down and put a cup of coffee before him on the kitchen table. 'Have you had lunch—can I get you anything to eat?'

'*Non, merci, mademoiselle*. I 'ave eaten in Rouen at the 'ospital. I come straight away from there.'

He gave Kate the news of Becky while he drank his coffee. She couldn't take in the details of the operation, especially as he used the French terms, but she gathered

that Becky had had a hysterectomy and that everything
had gone very well indeed. 'She came out of the an-
aesthetic beautifully and I was able to 'ave a little talk
with her just before I left,' he said with satisfaction. 'She
sends you her love and 'opes you are OK, and that the
manager for the 'otel arrived to take charge of
everything.'

Kate panicked. If the doctor knew the position here
and mentioned it to Becky, quite innocently, she dared
not think what harm it might do. It might even delay
her recovery if she knew that Kate was sharing the hotel
alone with a strange man who wasn't even the manager
person. She swallowed hard. 'Oh, yes, he came yesterday,' she said hastily, hoping fervently that Will would
keep out of the way.

But at that moment Will walked into the kitchen, a
piece of paper in his hand. Kate gave him a despairing
look. If only she'd had a moment to warn him, but now
it would all come out. She couldn't hope that Will would
interpret the message she was trying desperately to send
him.

The doctor held out a large hand to Will. 'You are
the young man who has come to look after the 'otel for
Madame Arnot, *oui*?'

'*C'est ça, monsieur*,' Will said with a small deferential bow. 'I do my best and *mademoiselle* is helping
me.'

'*Très bon, très bon*.' The doctor beamed. 'I will assure
madame that her 'otel is in good 'ands. And now I must
visit my patients.' He turned to Kate. 'I return to Rouen
later and telephone you this evening, *mademoiselle*, with
news of your aunt.'

'That would be very kind of you,' Kate said. 'Will
you please give her my love?' she added unsteadily. 'And
tell her I'll write.'

The little doctor bowed gallantly, thanked Kate for
the excellent coffee, and departed.

Will accompanied him to the door and Kate could hear him speaking in French to the doctor. Playing the manager, she thought. He had been very quick and plausible about accepting that role, hadn't he? She should be grateful—she *was* grateful. She wished she didn't feel vaguely uneasy about the facile way he'd entered into the deception.

He strolled back into the kitchen. '*Monsieur le docteur* was reassuring, don't you think? Do you feel better about things now? At least you know what's going on.'

Kate ran more hot water into the washing-up bowl. 'Thank you for covering up for me,' she said. 'You're very quick on the uptake.'

He grinned. 'It didn't stretch the old brain too much to guess that you didn't want your aunt to be bothered about the manager chap not turning up.'

She nodded, staring down into the bowl, swishing the suds around. 'Or about my staying here with a complete stranger. I wish I could see her and explain. Becky's only fiftyish, but in some ways she's still rather old-fashioned. She doesn't realise that girls have to learn to look after themselves these days.' She rattled a couple of plates down on the draining-board.

Will picked up a tea-towel and began to dry them absently. '*You've* learned very adequately,' he said, passing a finger over his mouth.

Kate ignored that. She said moodily, 'I hate telling lies. I much prefer always to tell the truth.'

Will said lazily. 'And what is the truth? You tell me. All the brightest brains have been arguing about it for about three thousand years and so far nobody has come up with the answer. For myself I believe that small lies are often necessary if you're not going to hurt people. Little white lies, they call them.'

'Perhaps,' she said grudgingly, 'but I still prefer to tell the truth.'

'Very admirable, I'm sure,' he mocked, stacking the clean plates neatly. 'And now, please, dear, clever Kate, will you come and fix those margins for me?'

Once Kate had solved the problem for him she pushed aside some of the mess of papers and books on the desk and settled down to write to Becky.

It was the most difficult letter she'd ever written in her life. She hated having to deceive Becky, but there was no help for it. The first part was easy—telling Becky about the doctor's visit and how kind he was, and how relieved she felt that the operation was successfully over.

I think about you all the time and hope everything will go well for you and that you won't be too un-comfortable. I would so love to be with you, but I know you feel that I shall be more useful keeping an eye on the hotel and the man who is helping to run it. He seems very capable and all is going well, so you mustn't worry about anything at all. Just give all your energy to getting well again. I send my best love and hope and see you before too long.

Your loving Kate.

She added a PS.

It wasn't necessary for me to move out and find another hotel, after all. I'm sure you'd agree that I'm in no danger from our temporary manager, if you could see him! He's not a bit dangerous and certainly not my type at all.

And that makes two more lies, she thought guiltily.

She sealed the letter, found stamps in a small box on the desk, and got to her feet. She glanced at Will, who was obviously deep in thought, staring at the computer screen. You didn't interrupt a writer of mysteries when he was trying to solve one. She scribbled on a piece of paper, 'Going to the village to buy bread. Will you hold the fort, please?' She put the slip beside him and walked out in silence.

It wasn't worth getting the car going—the village was only about half a mile away and she would enjoy the walk.

She remembered the village well, when she got there. It was tiny and very compact. Becky had explained how, in 1944, the landings of the Allied troops on the Normandy beaches had passed by, leaving it undamaged, unlike many villages nearer to the coast. Most of the small houses looked at least a hundred years old. They stood grouped round a central space where several small children played on a patch of bare ground. Unlike an English village, there were no front gardens—only window-boxes, which later in the season would be a blaze of colour.

Kate posted her letter and stood looking around. She remembered from a previous visit that the village, like most French villages, had its own *boulangerie* and, sure enough, attracted by the most wonderful smell of baking bread, she found it at the back of a cottage nearby.

She bought two extra-long *baguettes* and a couple of small apple tarts, which looked very tempting. The buxom lady behind the counter, whose English was better than Kate's French, recognised her, and Kate told her of Becky's illness.

She threw up her hands in horror. '*Ah—quel dommage*! Madame Arnot, she is a very nice lady.' She rattled on about Becky's popularity with the village folk and sent messages to her to get better very quickly.

Kate was warmed by the esteem in which Becky was evidently held in the village. She had a fleeting qualm of doubt about what the villagers would think if they knew that Becky's niece was alone with a strange man in the hotel. But perhaps they needn't know and Becky would soon be home herself and everything would be back to normal.

Thus reassuring herself, she went out into the sunshine again. Strolling along the dusty, narrow road, with
the sun warm on her cheeks, she felt a growing sense of
well-being. In a funny sort of way she was beginning to
enjoy her holiday, in spite of the inauspicious start.

Back at the hotel she was emptying the shopping bag
when Will put his head round the kitchen door. 'Good
smell,' he observed, eyeing the baguettes with approval.
'No phone calls while you've been out. I spotted the
postman and collected the letters from the box. Thought
I'd better start to establish myself as the manager. Two
bills and a letter from some people from Boulogne who
want to book for a week in August. Seems they are old
customers. We can deal with that together later. Oh, and
this letter came for you.' He handed her a large envelope. 'Are you feeling like tea?' he added wistfully.

Kate said, 'I certainly am. I'll make it now.'

'Give me a quarter of an hour and I'll be with you.'
Will limped back to the office.

Kate looked down at the letter. Edward's letter. She
hoped fervently that it was merely a friendly letter and
didn't suggest any change in their relationship. It would
be rather like Edward, she thought, to consider carefully
what he wanted to say and then write it down, rather
than blurt anything out on the spur of the moment.

It was a bulky envelope, and her heart sank as she
tore it open. It must be a very long letter—oh, dear!

But it wasn't a very long letter from Edward at all. It
was merely a note on one of the firm's 'with compliments' slips. Edward had written in his neat handwriting:

This came for you today. I hasten to send it on in case
it should be anything important. Best wishes, E.

Well, that was a relief, but who could have written to
her, care of Edward's firm?

She drew out the envelope inside and read, in a bold
black hand, 'Miss Katherine Lovell, c/o John Truslove

and Co', with the address of the firm in London. It was marked 'Please forward' in the top left-hand corner.

Kate held it in her hand and stared at it, weak with shock. She recognised that writing as well as she recognised her own name. A long time ago she had even been silly enough to copy his way of writing his 'y's—with a little twiddle on the tail. She walked stiffly over to the kitchen table and sat down. She wouldn't think about him—she *wouldn't*. She wouldn't even read the letter; she'd tear it up and forget it had ever come.

But remorselessly the memories returned, and now she couldn't hold them back. They ran through her mind as vividly as colour pictures on a screen. She was nearly fifteen and it was her first date and she'd been to a disco with Michael Brown, who was in the form above hers. She'd worn her peacock-blue dress and plaited her shining dark red hair in a new way she'd seen on TV. Michael had brought her home by half-past eleven, as promised, and he had kissed her goodnight on the doorsteps.

Pink-cheeked and starry-eyed, she'd walked into the living-room, to find Daddy alone, sitting by the fire. Mother had been out playing bridge. She played bridge three nights a week, and it hadn't seemed particularly odd that she and Daddy never seemed to go out together. When you were fourteen you grew up to accept these things as a matter of course.

He'd stood up when she went in and she had thought how handsome and wonderful he was, but that somehow he seemed sad tonight. Perhaps he was missing Mother. 'Here you are, then, Kathy. You look very beautiful. Had a good time?'

'Marvellous! Super!' She'd wanted to linger, to cheer him up, but at the same time she was impatient to be up in her own room to think about her evening and Michael's kiss. Her very first kiss!

'I'm off to bed; I've danced my feet off,' she'd said. She'd thought he looked disappointed, and impulsively she'd thrown her arms round his neck. 'Goodnight, Daddy. I do love you so much, my darling Daddy.'

He had hugged her back very tightly and held her away and looked into her face for a long time. 'And I love you, my Kathy. My beautiful grown-up daughter. Never doubt it.' He had kissed her forehead. 'Goodnight, Kathy.'

The next morning he had left on one of his trips abroad and she'd never seen him again.

More pictures came back as she stared at the envelope. Herself sitting at the kitchen table in the big house in Regent's Park, where they had lived then, pretending to do her maths homework, sensing that something was wrong, but not knowing what. Aunt Becky had arrived the day before from France and was in the dining-room, talking to Mother.

She could hear Becky's voice going on and on as she pressed home some argument. Mother and Becky always argued when they were together.

Never in her life had Kate listened at doors—the very idea was disgusting—but now, impelled by some force outside herself, she got up and walked into the hall.

The dining-room door was ajar and Becky's voice came clearly from inside the room. 'It's no good, Vera; James has left you. It's happened and you have to let yourself accept it, come to terms with it. Other women's husbands walk out on them; it happens all the time these days. James wasn't a bad man; I'm sure you'll find he's left you and Kate provided for. It'll all sort itself out.'

Then Mother's voice, hard and bitter, a voice that Kate didn't recognise. 'I shall sell the house and get a cheap flat somewhere and I shall find work. I'll give my life to Katherine. I'll work my fingers to the bone for her. And I'll do it alone.'

Kate felt the blood slowly draining from her body. It wasn't true; it couldn't be true. Daddy would never leave them; it was a bad dream. Her wonderful, adored father! She could hear his voice again saying, 'And I love you, Kathy. Never doubt it.'

She opened the door and saw the two of them, through a kind of mist—her mother, in a black dress, sitting straight up on a hard chair, Becky leaning towards her, hands on the polished table.

Their two faces were turned towards her. She ran across the room and threw herself down at Mother's feet, clutching at the smooth stuff of her dress. 'Mother, it's a mistake, isn't it? Tell me it's a mistake. Please, please tell me...' She was sobbing now, out of control. 'Daddy hasn't—hasn't left us, has he? *Has* he?'

Mother's face was a frozen mask. 'Oh, it's true, Katherine; your father has gone for good. There's only you and me now.'

'But how could he go—he wouldn't—he loves us.'

Mother's mouth twisted horribly. 'Oh, no, it seems he loves someone else.'

Becky came round the table, put her arms round Kate, and drew her to her feet. 'Come along with me, love; we'll make ourselves some tea.'

Dear, practical Becky, Kate thought now, remembering the horrible time that followed. Becky had done her best, but nothing could ease the pain. It was odd that it was Becky that she remembered. She could hardly remember Mother at all in those days—she had just been a sort of grey ghost, going grim-faced round the house, relentlessly cleaning and polishing everything in sight.

At first Kate wouldn't let herself believe it. Daddy would come back soon and everything would be the same as it had been before. But he hadn't come back. The house had been sold and a small flat in Hornsey bought with the proceeds. The balance of the sale money had been invested to produce enough income for them to live on. And as the weeks and months passed and she worked for her O levels, she had learned not to run to the door when she heard the postman, or listen for her father's step in the hall of the cramped little flat which had replaced the home she had grown up in and loved.

And the warm, adoring part of her heart which had once been her father's had grown into a frozen, empty place.

She had been so sorry for her mother, tried in her youthful way to make up to her for what she was doing, having supper ready when Mother got home late from the old folks' home where she worked all hours to make enough money to pay for little extras for Kate—pretty dresses, school holidays abroad. When Becky, on one of her frequent visits, had suggested that she apply for social security, she had drawn herself up in cold disdain. She would accept nobody's charity, she had declared proudly. She would be both father and mother to Katherine.

When the time came for Kate to apply for a place at college she had tried to persuade Mother not to work so hard, had pleaded to let her pay her own way, had offered to take a secretarial course instead of going to college, but Mother wouldn't hear of it. Even after Kate graduated and found her first job, Mother had gone on working. 'We still need the money,' she'd argued. 'We can move into a little house and get away from this dreary flat.'

On one occasion Kate and Becky had had words about it—the only time she had clashed with Becky. Kate had been worrying about Mother's health. 'She gets so tired. And she works far too hard in that home,' she'd said. 'She really doesn't need to keep the job now that I'm working. We could manage quite well on my salary.'

To her surprise Becky had been less than sympathetic. 'Let's face it, Kate dear,' she'd said wryly. 'Your mother's always enjoyed playing the martyr, you know.'

Shocked, Kate had rushed to Mother's defence. 'She doesn't have to play the martyr,' she'd burst out hotly. 'She *is* a martyr. Any woman is a martyr whose husband walks out and leaves her penniless with a young daughter to support. And she *has* supported me—she's given me everything.'

Becky had argued that Mother could have sued her husband for maintenance if she hadn't been so proud.

'Mother would never lower herself to do that,' Kate had said loyally, and Becky has shrugged and said, 'I suppose you're right, dear,' and the subject had never been mentioned again.

All so long ago and yet so fresh in her memory! Kate stared at the envelope on the table before her. Somehow he must know that Mother had died, and that she was alone now. Why else was he writing if not to ask her forgiveness, to try to make it up with her?

Oh, no, she thought bitterly, there's no forgiveness. Slowly, surely, Mother worked herself to death. You broke her heart and you broke her health and now you feel guilty and you come crawling back. I'll never forgive you, never, never, *never*. It took all the strength in her fingers to tear the letter, unopened, into half and then into half again, but she managed it at last. Then she found a box of matches, carried the pieces of the letter into the garden, and watched them burn.

As the heat ate through the layers the words 'your always loving Daddy' suddenly stood out with sickening clarity for a moment against the background of scorched paper before they disappeared in the flames.

When there was only a heap of ashes left, Kate ground it into the earth with her foot and went slowly back into the kitchen to put the kettle on for tea.

CHAPTER FOUR

KATE carried the tray into the office and put it down on the desk. 'I thought we might have a working tea,' she said, indicating the muddle of papers. If she could concentrate on the work of the hotel she might be able to get the bitter taste of the last few minutes from her mouth.

'Certainly.' Will swivelled his chair round from the computer table. 'At your service, *mademoiselle*.'

Kate couldn't summon up a smile. She poured out tea in silence and pushed a plate of Marie's almond cookies across the desk.

'Thanks.' Will munched thoughtfully. Then he said, 'What's the matter, Kate?'

She started. She'd forgotten how very perceptive he was. And the office overlooked the kitchen garden; he must have seen her burning the letter.

'Matter? Nothing's the matter, why should it be?'

He studied the ceiling. 'You receive a letter. A few minutes later you are seen cremating it in the garden with every sign of disgust and rejection. Following which you come in looking shell-shocked. Naturally, I'm a little perturbed.'

'You've been writing too many mysteries,' she snapped. 'And anyway it's got nothing to do with you.'

'That,' Will said suavely, 'is a matter of opinion.'

She began to lose her temper. 'Why can't you say what you mean, Will Raven? I'm getting a little tired of this double-talk.'

'OK, I will. The letter was from Edward—the nearly fiancé—was it?'

50

'Yes, it was from Edward. But it wasn't Edward's letter I was burning. There! Does that satisfy your beastly curiosity?'

'Then you're not thinking of—er—dispensing with Edward?'

Kate had reached the end of her patience. 'Look,' she exploded, 'why should you be so interested in my private affairs?'

'I'll tell you why.' Across the desk his dark eyes met hers and as she read the message in them she couldn't look away. Her breath caught in her throat and little tremors disturbed her inside.

'It was wishful thinking,' he said. A pause, and then, very slowly, 'You see, I find I'm—very interested in you, Kate.'

Nothing quite like this had ever happened to her before and she was at a loss as to how to deal with it. 'You don't . . . you can't . . .' she murmured feebly. 'And you promised——'

'Oh, don't worry, I'm not about to hurl myself across the desk and leap on you, although I should very much like to. Just that I hoped that the opposition had been removed. Is that truthful enough for you?'

At last she managed to wrench her eyes away. She took a gulp of tea and said, 'I think we'd better forget this conversation. Shall we get on with sorting out the letters and the books? If you're still willing to help, that is.'

'Of course I am,' he said, suddenly brisk, pulling the nearest pile of papers towards him. 'I'll translate them and you can decide what to do with them. OK?'

By the time the desk was cleared, and Kate was in the kitchen preparing the evening meal, she was almost able to see that disturbing small episode in its true light. Will hadn't meant to be taken seriously; his abrupt declaration was merely the result of proximity—as was her own response to that long, disturbing eye contact. He was a man; she was a girl. Just the usual physical attraction—nothing to get worked up about.

She sliced an onion and tossed the slices into a pan of sizzling oil. She certainly didn't intend to get involved with a man like Will Raven—casual, flippant, laid-back. He'd take his love-affairs like that, she felt sure; he wouldn't have a qualm about lying his way out of awkward situations if it suited him. Look how easily he'd justified passing himself off to Becky's doctor as the hotel manager! It had got her out of a difficulty, certainly, but she'd felt bad about it—whereas Will had certainly not shown any sign of conscience. Will told his 'little white lies' much too easily!

And when he'd said, 'I'm very interested in you', and looked so sincere, doubtless that was yet another 'little white lie.'

Kate was no moralist—certainly she never took exception to other people's morals, believing their lives were their own—but if she ever gave her heart to a man it would have to be a man she could admire as well as love, a man she could trust and believe in. That wasn't too much to ask, surely, even in the 1990s. Whenever she thought, however vaguely, about committing herself to any man, Mother's careworn face seemed to appear before her. She could hear Mother's sad voice saying shakily, 'Katherine, darling, don't make the mistake I made. When you marry, choose a man who is trustworthy and loyal.'

Which led her on to think about Edward. But for some reason she didn't want to think about Edward just now. Edward could wait until things had straightened themselves out here.

Will sauntered into the kitchen at that moment and came over to stand beside her at the sink. He was too near and she moved a fraction away.

'I smell something particularly scrumptious,' he murmured. 'Are we going to have a cordon bleu dinner?'

At the sound of a car at the front of the hotel he looked up. Then, 'Oh, my God, no!' he burst out in horror, staring sideways through the window at the gravel patch in front of the entrance door. 'She's run me to earth.'

Kate followed the direction of his look and saw a racy white MG pull up and a blonde young woman in a slinky black suit ease herself delicately out of the driving seat and stand gazing around her, the setting sun casting a rosy glow over her white-gold hair.

'Who?' Kate asked. She felt a sudden pang of something very like jealousy. Or perhaps it was merely feminine envy of another woman who could make such a spectacular entrance.

'Lisbeth, my agent.' Will sounded frantic. 'The very last person...' He grabbed Kate's arm and squeezed it tight. 'Kate, sweet Kate, you've got to help me,' he pleaded. 'I helped you, didn't I?'

The bell on the reception desk in the lounge pinged shrilly. 'I'll go,' Will said in a voice of doom.

'No, I'll go,' Kate said. 'This is a hotel and I'm in charge. Is she French—does she speak English?'

Will groaned. 'She's English, and she speaks it— fluently and incessantly.'

Seen close, the newcomer was even more spectacular. Her shining hair was expertly cut in a sideways sweep which almost covered one of her brilliant blue eyes. A gauzy scarf of exactly the same blue was draped with studied carelessness over her shoulders. An enormous silver brooch of Spanish design decorated the lapel of her black cashmere suit, which must have been custom-made in London. The black suede boots, one of whose pointed toes was tapping impatiently on the tiled floor, were certainly Italian, and the perfume that drifted round her whispered 'Paris'.

Quite a credit to the European Common Market, Kate thought sourly. 'Good evening, what can I do for you?' she said.

The woman tilted her head back and looked down her perfect small nose at Kate. 'Are you the receptionist at this—place?'

'I'm in charge of the hotel, yes,' Kate said shortly. 'But it's closed at present so I'm afraid I can't offer you accommodation.'

'I'm not looking for accommodation.' The dazzling blue eyes swept disdainfully over the cosy lounge with its well-worn chairs and wooden tables that bore the scars of long use. 'I'm looking for——'

She whirled round as Will came into the lounge. 'Will—darling!' Her voice changed, became syrupy. 'Then you *are* here—I couldn't understand why... Oh, my poor, sweet Will, what have you been doing to yourself?' She floated gracefully across the room and wound her arms round his neck, kissing him lingeringly on the mouth. 'I only got back from New York yesterday and I've been nearly going crazy with worry. I couldn't contact you anywhere; nobody seemed to know where you were. Eventually I rang Jimbo in Paris and he told me about your accident and that you'd been in hospital and gave me the address of this inn place where you were staying. I just had to jump in my car and drive over here straight away. I've got such a lot of news for you. What a time you must have had, poor darling, and are you better? Was it a broken leg and how did you do it? Come and sit down and take the weight off it and tell me all about it.' She linked her arm through his and guided him to a chair.

I don't believe it, Kate thought. But I know what Will meant by 'fluently and incessantly'. She would have very much liked to show this overwhelming young woman the door, but this was a hotel and Lisbeth was Will's agent, and had to be given a minimum of attention.

She walked across to the table where they were sitting. 'As I told you, the hotel is closed, but can I get you anything now you're here? A drink? Tea or coffee?'

Will met her eyes pleadingly. 'That's very kind of you, Kate. This is Lisbeth Brown, my literary agent. Lisbeth—Kate Lovell, who is looking after things here during her aunt's absence.'

Kate nodded and Lisbeth murmured, 'Hi!' without moving her limpid blue gaze from Will's face.

Will said, 'Perhaps we'd all like some coffee, Kate, if it's not too much trouble.'

'Of course not, Will,' Kate said sweetly and made for the kitchen.

In the kitchen Kate lowered the heat under the pan of onions and made a pot of coffee, trying to think what Will had meant when he'd said, 'You've got to help me'. Lisbeth was his literary agent, so possibly she had come to find out why he was not meeting the deadline for his book. That might explain his panic, but how could she, Kate, help him with that?

A more likely explanation was that Lisbeth was much more than a business colleague and was the suspicious type who would would be wildly jealous if she found out that Will was staying here alone with another woman. Yes, that was almost certainly the reason for his dismay.

Well, she could soon straighten that little matter out, Kate thought, as she carried the coffee tray back to the lounge.

Will got to his feet as she reached the table. 'Thank you, darling, that's fine. But you've only put two cups on the tray. You must join us.' His back was turned towards Lisbeth and he was pulling the most anguished face at Kate.

Lisbeth was saying, 'You can't stay in a place like this, Will—it's positively primitive. You need tender loving care. I shall put you in my car and drive you back home tomorrow. And then I can——'

'No, thanks, Lisbeth, I'm staying here.' Will managed to break into the monologue.

Something in his tone must have got through to Lisbeth. She raised her wonderfully blue eyes to his and for the first time she looked faintly puzzled.

'But Will—why?'

'Because I like it,' he said, 'and of course I wanted to be with Kate while she's here.' To Kate's utter astonishment he put an arm round her waist and drew her close against him, planting a kiss just below her ear.

If *she* was astonished, Lisbeth looked suddenly paralysed. Her vivid blue eyes stared, her pretty, painted mouth fell open, and the colour drained slowly away from her petal-soft cheeks.

Will sat down again. 'Have some coffee, Lisbeth,' he said, pouring out a cup and putting it before her. 'You've had a long drive. Have you had anything to eat? I'm sure Kate would rustle up something for you, wouldn't you, darling?'

Something laced with prussic acid would do nicely, Kate thought viciously. Not for poor, pretty Lisbeth, who looked shattered, but for the man who could so coldbloodedly and deviously deal her such a callous blow.

She gave him a cold, furious stare, walked back to the kitchen, and slumped into a chair, almost gibbering with rage and disgust.

Was this the way he finished his affairs? Hadn't he the decency to end them with compassion? There was something horribly familiar about the technique. The circumstances were different, of course, but she could almost feel the sick, empty horror of loss that poor Lisbeth was facing—the loss she herself had faced ten years ago. The heartless betrayal by someone who had professed to love you.

And to bring *her* into his nasty, lying ploy—to *use* her! It was quite unforgivable, and she wouldn't allow him to stay in this hotel another day. She would give him his marching orders straight away...

She was suddenly aware of an ominous smell of burning issuing from the cooker. She sprang to her feet. Thick blue smoke was rising from the frying pan and the onions were reduced to a gooey black mess. She switched off the hotplate, picked up the pan-holder, and dropped the pan and its contents into the sink, where it hissed and spluttered angrily.

It just needed this, Kate thought, leaning on the sink as fumes from the burning onions stung her eyes and tears rolled down her cheeks.

'What on earth's going on?' Will's voice came from behind her. 'Are you trying to burn the place down now?'

He sounded irritable. What right had *he* to be irritable, the lying cheat?

'Go away,' Kate choked, one hand to her mouth. 'Go back to your ladyfriend.'

He leaned down and peered at her face. 'You're crying—what's the matter?' He looked down at the pan, which was still sizzling in the sink. 'You picked that up, you little idiot? Didn't you see that the handle is made of metal? You've burned yourself. Here, put your hand under the cold tap.' He grabbed her wrist and held her hand in the flow of icy water.

'It's all right—it's nothing.' Kate tried to disengage her hand from his grasp, but he was much too strong and she had to submit. When at last he turned off the tap her whole hand was numb.

'Come and sit down.' He pushed her into a chair. 'A first-aid box?'

'In the cupboard over there, But, really, I'm all right—there's no need...'

It was no good arguing with him, and, to tell the truth, Kate was enjoying the feeling of his fingers on her hand as he smoothed on cream from a tube.

'I think it's only superficial, but we'll see how it goes,' he said. 'You must rest for a bit—come back into the lounge and lie on the sofa. I put some more logs on the fire; it's nice and warm in there.'

Kate was pulling herself together rapidly. 'I'll go up to my room,' she said, a chill in her voice. 'I don't care to take part in any more of your disgusting charades for the benefit of your agent—or your lover—or whatever she is.'

'Certainly not my lover and never has been, thank God,' Will said fervently. 'Although that's been Lisbeth's hope for some time past. Anyway, don't worry, she's left—gone off to friends in Paris. I don't think she's very pleased with me just now. She'll come round soon— she makes quite a bit of money out of me, so she can't afford to stay on her high horse for long.' He chuckled.

The picture of a sobbing, heartbroken rejected lover facing a black future was rapidly fading from Kate's mind. Instead there was an odd feeling of gratification that Lisbeth wasn't Will's girlfriend, only his agent.

'All the same, I don't like being taken for granted and used like that,' she muttered as he put a strong arm round her and led her back to the lounge, settling her on the sofa. The room looked cosy and welcoming. The daylight was beginning to fade and the log fire was glowing brightly.

Will went out of the room, returning with a warm coverlet from his own bed. He lifted her legs on to the sofa and tucked them up carefully. 'Keep the patient warm and reassured,' he murmured. 'First rule in treatment for shock. How am I doing?'

'Didn't you hear what I said?' Kate made her voice severe. The sensation of having Will's arm round her, Will's hands touching her, had been much too disturbing. He had a dangerously magnetic physical attraction, she admitted; she had to watch herself.

'About taking you for granted and using you?' He sank down on to the rug before the fire, and leaned back against the side of the sofa. 'Kate, my darling, I would never take you for granted—never. As for using you—well, maybe I reckoned you owed me that in return for your use of me for the doctor's benefit.'

'Another "little white lie"?' Kate said slowly. 'We seem to be making a habit of telling them. I still don't like it.'

He shrugged. 'It seemed a marvellous opportunity to show Lisbeth kindly but beyond a doubt that she was wasting her time.'

Kate said cautiously, 'She's very beautiful; I wonder you wanted to discourage her.'

He grinned. 'Very beautiful—and made of sheet metal under the gloss. Useful for an agent, perhaps, but I imagine somewhat painful in bed.'

In spite of herself, Kate burst out laughing.

'That's better,' Will said cheerfully, reaching up and laying a finger on the bandaged hand. 'How does it feel?'

'Fine. It hardly hurts at all.' By now, she had only the merest qualm of conscience about her imaginary injury. It was far too tempting to let him make a fuss of her.

'Good. Well, you stay here and make pictures in the fire and I'll go and do my chef act. I have two specialties—scrambled eggs and Welsh rarebit. What is your choice, *mademoiselle*?'

'Oh, Welsh rarebit—lovely. But I could perfectly well——'

She started to get up, but Will was on his feet in an instant, pushing her down firmly but gently, both hands on her shoulders. 'Do as you're told, girl. I'm in charge at the moment. Shan't be long.' He leaned over and planted a kiss on her hair. 'Your hair's like burnished copper in the firelight,' he said softly, and limped out of the room.

Kate stayed where she was, her heart beating erratically. Will was a lightweight; she mustn't allow herself to fall for his charm. She must think about Edward, which was what she had planned to do while she was here.

Edward was a solid citizen; he would make a good husband and father. Not exciting, perhaps, but kind, trustworthy, faithful. Above all, faithful—she was sure of it. She knew all about the other kind; she had watched Mother gradually going downhill year after year. Oh, yes, she knew about faithless husbands, and the misery they caused. Not for her the charming, amusing Will Ravens of this world, who would pass from one woman to another without a qualm. She'd watched him at work today. He'd said that he and Lisbeth had never been lovers, but could she believe him? A lie meant nothing to him; he'd said so. 'All in a good cause,' he would say lightly.

She stared into the fire and did her best to see Edward's face, but it eluded her. She must try to feel a little closer to him. She would write to him tomorrow, a nice friendly letter that would be waiting for him when he came back from Yorkshire. He would appreciate that.

Will appeared in record time, bearing their supper on two small trays. He put one on Kate's knees, the other on a low table beside the sofa, and pulled up a fireside chair.

'How about that, then?' he grinned. 'Five-star service. I took the liberty of raiding the cellar, too, is that OK?' He poured red wine into two glasses.

The Welsh rarebit tasted wonderful, the cheese faintly browned on the top and still bubbling beneath. Kate discovered that she was starving as she tucked into it. Her green eyes twinkled back at him. 'My compliments to the chef. It's a masterpiece—just the right amount of mustard and Worcestershire sauce!'

They ate in companionable silence and finished off with crisp green apples. Will removed their trays and came back with coffee.

'This is luxury,' Kate sighed. 'I'm not used to being waited on.'

Will leaned back in his chair. 'You live alone since your Mother died? Whereabouts?'

'It's a small flat—in Hornsey,' she told him. 'I'm going to sell it if I can, and find something——' she hesitated '—more convenient.' Unless, of course, she married Edward.

He nodded. 'Your job's in the City?'

'Was,' Kate told him. 'I'm between jobs just now. The last one was temporary, and that suited me because my mother needed nursing.' She added soberly, 'I hoped we could pull her through, but it wasn't to be. She had a bout of flu just after Christmas and it turned to pneumonia. She wasn't very strong and it was—too much for her.' She stared into the fire, remembering the pinched face and careworn hands.

'I'm sorry,' Will said quietly. 'It must have been a bad time for you.'

After a silence he said, 'Tell me some more about yourself, Kate. I want to know all about you.'

She turned her head and met his eyes. They looked inky-black in the firelight. 'Why?' she said.

She knew as soon as she said it that it was a leading question—most unwise of her, especially after his surprising protestation earlier.

Still in that deep, quiet voice he said, 'Because we're friends, aren't we? Friends like to know about each other.'

Friends? Well, yes, she supposed she could accept that. 'There isn't much to know,' she said. 'I'm just an ordinary girl.'

'That I would dispute,' he said. 'But never mind that. Tell me about your job—where you work, what you do in your spare time, how many boyfriends you have, what you like to read, what music you listen to, whether you prefer the town to the country...oh, everything.'

Kate smiled weakly. 'That's a tall order. As I said, I'm between jobs at present, I haven't had any spare time recently, boyfriends ditto. Except Edward, of course, and I haven't known him very long.'

'But you're nearly engaged?' He was watching her closely.

She nodded. 'That's the idea.'

'Yours—or Edward's?'

'I'll pass on that one,' she said. 'Let's go on—I like any sort of music, according to my mood, and the same with books. Although I'm quite a push-over for mysteries—does that make you feel good?'

He grinned. 'It makes me shake in my shoes,' he admitted.

'And that,' Kate told him, 'is undoubtedly another of your famous "little white lies"—disguised as modesty. I'm sure you're delighted with your own books; you wouldn't be human if you weren't. May I know what name you write under?'

He hesitated.

'Come *on*,' Kate chivvied him. 'Friends like to know about each other—wasn't that the idea?'

'Oh, well,' he said at last, reluctantly, 'nothing very earth-shaking. The name's Martin Shaw.'

'Oh! You're Martin Shaw! But I *dote* on Martin Shaw. I've read all of them, every single one.'

Will pulled a face. 'I'm glad—that's very flattering. But——' he hesitated again '—I'd much rather you doted on Will Raven, you know.'

Kate burst out laughing. 'You never miss a trick, do you?'

He sighed. 'What can I do to make you take me seriously?' He got up from his chair and edged himself on to the sofa beside her. 'Perhaps if I kissed you again— only differently this time?'

His arm wound itself round her. His mouth was very close to hers. Kate was conscious of a reckless kind of desire beating inside her. He was very sweet... What harm was there in a kiss? It was a natural thing to happen. He waited for a moment to give her time to draw away, and when she didn't his mouth came down to hers in a gentle kiss that flicked across her lips as delicately as a butterfly's wing.

Suddenly she knew for the first time what it meant to feel the earth moving beneath her. Her left arm went up and round his neck and she opened her lips to his with a little sigh of pure desire.

'Oh, Kate—oh, my darling girl,' he murmured against her mouth, and his kiss deepened, his tongue searched for hers and found it, and she lay back and sank into the wonder of new, throbbing, heart-shaking sensations as his lips moved to an erotic place behind her ear, and then began to slide downwards.

She felt his fingers quickly unbuttoning her blouse and was helpless to stop them. She was even shamelessly glad that there was no bra to hide her swelling breast from his mouth. She let out a little cry at the sudden intense pleasure as his mouth closed over the hardened peak, his tongue flicking and stroking until she felt her whole body begin to melt.

Then, as quickly as it had started, it was over. Clumsily he drew the fronts of her blouse together and slid off the edge of the sofa on to the floor with a thump, where he sat motionless, his head in his hands.

At last he pulled himself up with a deep sigh and sank into his easy-chair. 'Sorry, Kate,' he said. 'My fault. I shouldn't have let that happen. It was too much—too soon—too complicated.'

Too complicated! It was as if he had slapped her in the face. That could only mean one thing—that he owed his loyalty to another woman. Not Lisbeth, but some unknown woman. Kate felt a wave of self-disgust wash over her. How could she have behaved so—so wantonly? She struggled to restore the situation. 'I shouldn't have thought it was very complicated,' she said, trying to sound amused and not succeeding very well. 'Just a kiss between friends—nothing much in that.'

'Is that what it meant to you—"nothing much"?'

She gulped. 'That's right.'

He leaned towards her and his eyes were like pools of dark water in the glint of the firelight. 'Oh, Kate,' he said reproachfully, 'who's telling little white lies now?'

She was speechless. He was right, of course, that kiss had meant much more than a friendly caress. For the first time in her life she had been carried away on a surging wave of passion.

He said, 'Would you like me to leave?'

Kate felt the blood drain away from her cheeks. 'Yes—no—I don't know.' She couldn't think—she could only feel, and what she felt was frightening and confusing and somehow wonderful.

It was quite dark outside the window now. Will got up, switched on the wall-lights round the room, and pulled the flower-patterned curtains.

'Firelight's too damned seductive,' he said, coming back to his chair. He smiled at her ruefully. 'Well, Miss Katherine Lovell, we seem to have a slight problem. What are we going to do about it?'

'Why ask me?' Kate came back at him, trying to sound as if nothing out of the ordinary had happened. 'Surely you're the one to "do something about it". You started it. OK, so I didn't stop you. As you said, firelight's se-ductive. We must take care to keep all the lights on in future. That is——' she hesitated '—unless you really want to leave.'

He glared at her angrily. 'I do *not* want to leave, you know darned well I don't,' he said, and Kate had to sup-press the sudden rush of relief she felt.

There was a small silence and when he spoke again it was quietly, candidly. 'You've half converted me to telling the truth, Kate, so here it is: I very much want

to make love to you. I'm tempted to try to persuade you
to agree, but I promised not to take advantage of your
situation here, and I intend to keep that promise. Does
that satisfy you?'

'Satisfy?' Didn't he know the only thing that would
satisfy them both? Yes, of course he did, but he had
chosen to keep a promise and she respected him for that.

Another lie was required of her now, and this time
not so little, not so white. She bent her head so that he
couldn't see her eyes. 'That satisfies me,' she said.

CHAPTER FIVE

WILL stood up. 'I'll be in the office,' he said gruffly. 'I've got work to finish.'

As he walked to the door his limp seemed more pronounced and Kate felt an odd tug in the region of her heart. She had a sudden urge to go after him and say she would agree to anything he wanted. That was the stark truth. Whether she liked it or not she wanted nothing more than to go back into his arms. But it was only a physical thing—for both of them. Nothing to do with love—real, lasting love that she could give herself to whole-heartedly. She would never settle for less. And where did that leave Edward? That was a question she had to face.

The sound of the phone ringing in the office put an end to her musings. Could it be the doctor, so soon? She pushed back the coverlet and ran into the office.

Will was perched on the edge of the desk, the receiver to his ear. He put a hand over the mouthpiece. 'The doctor,' he whispered to Kate. She watched his face, anxiously, trying to read the message, but his expression told her nothing.

When the conversation seemed to be coming to an end she put in quickly, 'Ask him when Becky can see visitors.'

He nodded and spoke again, listened, and, finally, with *'Très bien. Merci, monsieur, au revoir,'* he replaced the receiver.

He smiled down into Kate's questioning face. 'All's going very well—no problems. You can see your aunt tomorrow if you wish. She has a room to herself and you can visit at any time.'

'Oh, marvellous.' Kate sighed with relief. 'I'll leave straight after breakfast.'

'Driving?' said Will.

'Why, yes, of course.'

'You know Rouen? You can find your way to the hospital?'

'Of course I can,' she said firmly. But her heart sank at the prospect when she came to consider it. She had got lost twice in Rouen on her way here, and the thought of trying to find the hospital when she wouldn't even be able to understand the replies to her halting enquiries was daunting.

She bit her lip, fighting down her annoyance.

As usual, Will read her thoughts. 'I could be your chauffeur if I hadn't got a gammy left leg. Just now I wouldn't be safe behind a wheel. We'll have to think of something else. I suppose you don't drive an automatic, by any chance?'

Kate shook her head. 'No, but Becky has a Renault—rather old. I seem to remember that it has an automatic drive.'

'Let's go and see. Come on—never admit defeat.'

Sure enough, the big black car in the garage proved to be an automatic, and Bill soon got the engine running. 'Hop in,' he told Kate, switching on the headlights. 'We'll have a run round to try her out. I must be sure I'm safe to handle her.'

He drove along the lane and out into the main road for several miles, then turned and drove back, professing himself delighted with the car and his own confidence in driving it. 'Great!' he enthused, running the car into the garage. 'We'll start out after breakfast, shall we?'

'Well, it's good of you to offer,' Kate said doubtfully, 'but how about leaving the phone?' There had already been several calls, one of them a fortnight's booking for a family of four. 'I wouldn't want to miss anything important.'

'Easy,' he said. 'We use the *répondeur*. That'll take care of it.'

'*Répondeur*?' Kate queried.

'Answerphone to you,' he replied with a grin.

Kate felt somewhat deflated as they walked back to the hotel. Her self-image of confidence was being seriously undermined by this man. She wasn't exactly a feminist, but she liked to believe she could pull her weight in most situations.

'You think of everything, don't you?' she said. And in case that sounded too ungracious she added, 'I don't know how I should get along without you. I suppose one day I'll learn to find my own way about in this foreign land. It must be satisfying to be bilingual. Or do you have other languages?'

'German—Spanish—sketchy Italian,' he admitted.

'There's modesty for you!' Kate mocked. 'You must have been a horrid little swot at school.'

'Not at all. Horrid, probably, but certainly not a swot. Languages are a gift—like an ear for music, or your prowess with a computer.'

This easy banter lasted until they were back in the hotel.

Kate locked the front door. 'I think I'm for bed,' she said, trying to sound ordinary. The warm intimacy of the lounge, with the sofa drawn up before the glowing embers of the log fire, was doing disturbing things to her breathing.

'You wouldn't like a night-cap?' Will suggested.

She shook her head, turning to the stairs.

'Kate!' He put a hand on her arm. 'Don't be scared—I won't let it happen again.'

She searched his face with troubled eyes, but could see nothing there that reassured her. He was an enigma.

'Goodnight, Will,' she said. 'Switch off all the lights, won't you?' And she went quickly up the stairs.

If things had been different Kate would have enjoyed the drive to Rouen next morning through the Normandy countryside, with its tree-lined fields and placid black and white cows. But as it was she was too tired and confused to notice much of it. She had spent a restless night, sleeping in snatches, arguing with herself every time she wakened. Common sense told her what she ought to do about Will Raven, if she was going to have any peace of mind. She ought to send him away. She wasn't a child; she was a woman of twenty-five, and she was perfectly well aware of what had happened last night. She had heard about it—read about it—that hot rush of sheer sensuality which had nearly overcome her in Will's arms. But she had never imagined it would happen to her. It had been all the more overwhelming because she had considered herself a cool, sensible girl, well in control of her emotions.

Will had made no secret of the fact that she attracted him, and it was quite possible that he would make a serious pass at her, in spite of his promise. Especially as his other woman, whoever she was, wasn't available. If he did, Kate wasn't at all sure how her body would react, and if she would be able to control it. And to enter into any sort of relationship with him would be unthinkable. Not for her the charming, amusing Will Ravens of this world—she knew only too well the damage and heartache they caused. She could never forget the casual way her father had walked out on his responsibilities.

Yes, the safest thing would be to send Will away. On the other hand, she couldn't do without his help. She couldn't possibly look after the hotel on her own, not knowing the language. Perhaps he really meant what he said last night, that he wouldn't let it happen again. She'd have to hope that for once in his life he was telling the truth.

Will himself seemed totally unaware of her troubled state of mind. He was looking rather fabulous this morning, Kate had to admit, glancing up at him. He had exchanged his 'student' gear for a clean white shirt and black trousers. The sunlight glinted on his dark hair and as he narrowed his eyes against the light his amazing lashes looked even longer than she had noticed at first.

'Enjoying it?' he asked, as the Renault ate up the miles. 'It's a super morning, isn't it? You're very silent, Kate. Not worrying about your aunt, are you? I'm sure she'll be OK.' He put a sympathetic hand on her knee briefly.

Kate's inside quivered. Damn the man, why did he have to touch her? 'I'll be happier when I've seen her. Can we stop somewhere to buy flowers, please?'

'Of course. I know just the place, no problem.'

He drove the big car confidently and not too fast for Kate's nerves. She had been half afraid he would turn out to be a showy driver and was relieved that he wasn't.

When they reached the city Kate was very glad that Will was driving. 'I got horribly lost here on my way from London,' she confessed. 'I seemed to be going round and round and it was more by good luck than anything else that I found myself on the right road at last.'

'Rouen's not the most driver-friendly town,' Will said. 'You would probably come in from the old town and would have to cross one of the bridges. The part we're going through now is known as the new town. This is where all the administration and business goes on. Most of the buildings are somewhat soulless.' He nodded towards an enormous white structure. 'But wait until we get across the river into the old town—it's quite different. The hospital's over on that side too.'

Once across the River Seine it was like being in a different world. As they drove along, Kate peered up narrow streets with fascinating old houses. 'I'd love to stop and wander round when we've been to the hospital,' she said.

'I'd love to take you,' Will agreed enthusiastically. 'We'll take a look at the cathedral and pick up lunch somewhere.'

He drove to a shopping area, where Kate bought a bunch of spring flowers for Becky. They then continued on their way to the hospital.

When the car was parked she followed him inside, where the layout seemed bewilderingly complicated, with signs that she didn't understand.

'I'm in your hands,' she admitted. 'I'd be lost here in minutes.'

'Trust me,' he said, approaching the reception desk.

Butterflies fluttered in Kate's stomach as she and Will trailed along endless passages, past hurrying nurses, porters wheeling trolleys and doctors in long white coats deep in conversation together. At last the nurse who had been guiding them stopped outside a door. 'Madame Arnot,' she announced, adding something in French.

Kate looked at Will questioningly. 'She says not more than five minutes, and only one at a time. Your aunt is still somewhat weak.'

The nurse opened the door for Kate to enter. 'Stay here,' she whispered to Will. 'I'd never find my way out again by myself.'

'Of course,' he said. He leaned back against the wall and folded his arms. 'Good luck.'

Kate's heart was beating nervously fast as she went into the small white room, rather dreading what she might see. Becky had always been so healthy and energetic that it was difficult to think of her as an invalid. She needn't have worried. The Becky resting back against the pillows in the hospital bed was the Becky of old. A little paler, a little thinner, but all the exuberance of the old Becky was there.

Kate put down her bunch of spring flowers beside a vase of red rosebuds on the locker and kissed her. 'How are you, Becky? I've been so worried about you.'

'Kate! Dearest girl, how lovely to see you! They sent a message up from Reception to say you were here. I'm absolutely tip-top. Everybody's been so kind.' She saw Kate glanced at the red rosebuds on the locker and her cheeks turned slightly pink. 'Those are from my faithful doctor friend. He's such a poppet. But don't let's talk about me. I want to hear everything you've been doing, and what's been happening at my beloved Ferme.'

Kate pulled up a chair and sat down beside the bed, holding Becky's hand. She was going to have to use some of Will's little white lies now. 'Everything's been going swimmingly,' she said. 'There've been three bookings since you left and quite a bit of correspondence, which I've turned over to——' she swallowed '—to our temporary manager.'

'Ah, yes, Monsieur Boudin. I'm glad he arrived on time. I was rather perturbed when you said in your letter that you'd decided to stay on at the Ferme while he was there, but I'm sure your judgement is sound, Kate. You're a sensible girl. You get on well with our Monsieur Boudin, do you?' She chuckled. 'Do you know what *boudin* means in English? It means a black pudding or a kind of sausage. I see him as plump and middle-aged and cheery. Am I right?'

Kate nearly choked. 'Well, not really, but he's very capable.' She changed the subject hastily. 'I'm having a lovely restful holiday and I've been to the village. The bakery lady sends her love and good wishes. I'll get out in the car now and again, but I'll certainly stay on until you're home again. I'm sure I'll be able to help.'

'If you're really sure...' Becky said doubtfully, but she looked delighted. 'That would be marvellous.

Jacques and Marie will be back in about ten days and we can have some time together.'

Kate asked, 'When do you think they'll let you out?' That might be tricky. She'd have to hope the real Pierre Boudin turned up by then.

'In three or four days, it seems. They don't keep you in any longer than necessary. But Louis—that's my doctor friend—insists on arranging for me to spend a week or so at his home near Caen. His sister lives with him and she and I get on very well indeed. Louis says that if I return to the hotel too soon I will try to overdo things.' She pulled a face. 'It's strange to be looked after again—but rather nice, I must admit. The good thing is that it will be nearer for you, and perhaps you'll be able to visit.'

'Of course,' Kate said, hoping she didn't sound suspiciously relieved that Becky would be away for some time longer.

She thought Becky was looking a little tired and said, 'Now, is there anything I can do for you before I go? Anything you need?'

'Nothing, dear, nothing at all. Louis keeps me supplied with books, and he's even arranged to have my laundry done.' She laughed rather self-consciously. 'It's very useful to have a doctor friend if one has to be ill.'

Kate stood up. 'Extremely useful,' she said with a teasing smile. 'I shall want to hear all about him next time I visit.'

She kissed Becky goodbye and Becky clung on to her for a moment longer. 'It's been super seeing you, Kate, dear. So clever of you to find me. Rouen's rather muddy for driving. Did you manage it all right?'

Another lie was more than Kate could bring herself to tell. 'Oh, our friendly manager offered to drive me, so I accepted. My French is appalling, as you know, and I thought it would be easier. We left your answerphone primed so there won't be any messages missed.'

'The little sausage! Do ask him to come in for a moment or two, Kate. I should very much like to see him—to assure myself that he's the right type to have charge of the Ferme.'

Kate went cold all over. If Becky saw Will Raven—youngish and handsome, and devastatingly sexy—all would be lost. Goodness knew what harm it might do.

'I-I'm not sure where he is,' Kate said vaguely.

'Well, do try, there's a kind girl,' Becky urged. 'It would speed my recovery if I just set eyes on him for a few minutes.'

'I'll see if I can find him,' Kate said, kissing Becky again. 'He may have gone back to the car.'

She went out and closed the door, leaning against it, breathing as if she'd been running a marathon. Will was still propped up against the wall where she had left him, arms folded. He looked quite fabulously attractive, Kate had to admit. Anything less like a sausage she couldn't imagine, she thought, feeling like bursting into mad laughter.

'All OK?' He stepped forward.

'Ssh! Don't let her hear you. She's got the idea that she wants to see you. She thinks you're Pierre Boudin, of course. I'll just pop my head round the door and say I can't find you.'

She reached for the door-handle, but Bill pulled her arm back. 'No—don't,' he said rather peremptorily. 'I'd very much like to have a word with *madame*. Don't worry, Kate, all will be well.'

'Oh, it won't, it won't; it'll spoil everything. Please don't go in. Please.'

'I want to,' Will said firmly. 'You stay here.' He opened the door, walked in, and closed it again.

Kate stood glaring at the closed door, bubbling with rage and impotence. How dared he barge in like that? But the damage was done now; she couldn't go in after him and create a scene in Becky's room. She had to wait helplessly while he did untold harm in there. Becky wasn't easily fooled; she wouldn't be taken in by his lies. The sheer arrogance of the man, she fumed, to think he could win over a woman of Becky's experience and good sense!

Kate had never been so blindingly angry in her life. This was the end, the very last time she'd let him smooth-talk her into letting him 'help' her. She'd manage on her own from now on and he could jolly well clear out.

Her knees were buckling under her and she staggered along the passage and sank on to a bench. It was her own fault; this was what came from entering into a stupid deception, however good the excuse was. Fool—idiot— she accused herself. She should never had let the man stay, never have been won over by his undoubted charisma.

She kept looking towards the closed door, biting her lip. He must have been in there more than five minutes, surely? What was going on? She had horrid pictures of Becky collapsing from shock at finding she had been deceived by Kate—someone she loved and trusted. If she'd been in her usual robust health she could have coped, but after a major operation...

At last the door opened and closed and Will came along the passage to her. He was grinning widely. 'I think I made quite a hit,' he said smugly. '*Madame* approves of me. 'I've convinced her that her hotel—and her niece—are safe in my hands.'

Kate sprang to her feet. 'I don't believe it,' she spat. 'What lies have you been telling her?'

'I suppose you wouldn't believe that I didn't need to tell her any lies.'

'No, I wouldn't. I'm going in again to see what state she's in.' She raced down the passage to the door, but the nurse, coming from the other direction, was there before her.

'*Non, non.*' She held up a hand, smiling, and added something in French.

Kate frowned up at Will, who was close behind her.

'Nurse says she can't possibly allow any more visiting today,' he said.

'Oh, please,' Kate begged the nurse. 'Just for a minute.' She made a grab at the door-handle, but Will pulled her away firmly.

'Come along, Kate, there's a good girl. Never argue with a senior nurse.'

He took her arm in an iron grip and forced her, gibbering with rage, back along the route they had come, and out to the car park. There he pushed her, none too gently, into the waiting car.

'Let's find somewhere for lunch,' he said, ignoring her spluttering protests. 'I seem to remember there's a nice little café somewhere near the cathedral.'

'No!' Kate yelled. 'I don't want lunch. Why won't you listen to me? I want to know what story you told Becky. She must have been shocked out of her mind when she saw you. She couldn't have believed you're a hotel manager. And I'd given her the impression you were Pierre Boudin—and she expected to see something like a—a—sausage—and—and—I'm sure she's horribly upset—and she'll never forgive me.' Her throat choked up humiliatingly. 'Oh, it's all so—so—beastly. I don't know why I agreed to let you stay. And don't touch me.'

She jumped as Will switched off the engine and slid a comforting arm round her shoulders.

'Just calm down, sweetheart,' he soothed. 'You really mustn't take things so seriously. I promise you that your Aunt Becky is quite happy with the situation.'

She wriggled away from him. 'Promise! You! What are your promises worth?'

'Listen!' Will roared, so fiercely that the breath almost left Kate's body. 'I thought it best to get this situation straightened out. Whether you believe me or not, I told your aunt the plain truth. I told her who I was and exactly what had happened. I explained that we had kept the details from her because you were afraid she might be upset about the hitch in her plans, when she was undergoing an operation.' In the same matter-of-fact voice he went on, 'I also assured her that she mustn't worry about you—that I'd never hurt you in any way, because I happen to have fallen in love with you. I'm glad to say that Becky seemed quite happy with the idea—and I hope you will be eventually. At least, it should clear away the guilty feeling you seem to be suffering from.'

Kate sagged against the car seat, pushing back her mane of dark red hair with shaking fingers. She felt like a character in a cartoon when a streamroller has flattened it. 'You—you're incredible,' she muttered. 'I don't know what to say.'

'Then don't say anything,' Will told her briskly. 'Let's find a cheerful place to eat. I'm hungry.'

Kate felt confused, relieved—and curiously excited. But that was the effect Will always seemed to have on her. She sighed. 'OK, you win. That sounds like a good idea.'

Now that he had won the small battle Will was all geared for action.

'I suggest we leave the car here and walk,' he said. 'It's not far to the centre of the town and the car park's bound to be full.'

Kate was in a mood to agree to anything by now. He locked the car and linked his arm with hers in a companionable way, and they set off.

'All the interesting monuments are around here,' Will told her, 'including the cathedral, which is famous for its spire. It's supposed to be the tallest in France, or is it in the world?'

'I wouldn't know,' said Kate absently. She was listening with only a quarter of her mind to Will's tourist spiel. The other three-quarters were busy trying to work out how he had managed to convince Becky of his credentials and his integrity in so short a time—if indeed he had, she thought darkly.

But as they strolled along the narrow streets Kate put her suspicions behind her. Will knew Rouen well and he pointed out the the Renaissance churches, the fabulous Palais de Justice, the great old houses that had been war damaged and meticulously restored.

'But the jewel in the crown is the cathedral,' he said. 'Superb, don't you think?'

They had arrived at the centre of the old town and the cathedral soared gracefully above them, thrusting its lacy spire into the puffy blue and white clouds.

'You have to forget about the scaffolding,' Will said sadly. 'At least it's a sign that the cathedral will survive into the future.'

'It's marvellous,' Kate breathed. 'Quite fantastic! I've seen pictures of it, of course, but they don't give you a true idea of the real thing.'

'And the truth is what Kate appreciates,' Will teased, reaching out to twist back a strand of her richly red hair which had come loose in the breeze.

'Of course.' She grinned up at him, and suddenly she felt her worries slipping away as their eyes met. Perhaps things were taking a turn. Becky was out of danger and recovering rapidly, and she had no choice but to take Will's word for it that she had accepted his explanation. Becky must be more trusting than I am, Kate thought. But then, Becky had never been betrayed by someone she loved and trusted with all her heart and soul. She thrust the bitter memory away. If Becky could accept Will Raven's word then she must try to do the same.

He was still drinking in the view. 'Did you know that Monet painted fifty pictures of the cathedral? He had lots of them on the go at once, and each time the light changed—morning, afternoon and evening—he'd move from one to the other and go on working. The mind boggles! I wish I could work on fifty mystery books at once. I'd be a millionaire in no time.' His dark eyes danced in the sunlight; his mouth was tilted upwards. He really was fun to go out with, Kate admitted. She couldn't remember the last time she'd felt so young and light-hearted.

'Am I boring you about art and artists?' he said. 'It's my pet hobby—art history. Some time ago I had to do some research for a book and I got hooked on it.'

Kate shook her head. 'You're not boring me a bit,' she told him. 'I'm interested, but very ignorant.' If he talked about art it would steer the conversation away from more dangerously personal channels.

'I've always intended to take time off to explore inside the cathedral,' he said, 'but somehow I've never got around to it when I've happened to be in Rouen.' He linked an arm through hers and gave it a little squeeze. 'Let's play truant and do the thing properly together one day, when we haven't got the hotel to think about, shall we?'

It was such a small, friendly gesture, and the words were merely friendly too, but taken together they gave the impression of a shared future, which was, Kate tried to assure herself, not in her scheme of things at all. She had to ignore the little warm tug in the region of her heart.

After some searching Will found a small café which provided a view of the cathedral. Except for a few tourists the café was empty and they sat in a window table with a yellow cloth. Will shrugged off his red ski-jacket and tossed it down. Out of force of habit, Kate arranged it neatly on the back of his chair, and immediately felt self-conscious about the wifely gesture. 'Nice cheerful colour,' she said hastily.

'I'm a nice cheerful fellow, hadn't you noticed?' He glanced up at the menu on the wall. 'What would you like to eat?' he asked.

'What can you get here?'

'Well, you can usually get a *croque monsieur*.'

'Sounds fun—what is it?'

He grinned. 'Well, it's the French version of your favourite Welsh rarebit.'

She smiled back. 'Yummy!'

While they ate, Will talked about Monet and his famous garden at Giverny and his pictures of water-lilies, and Kate listened and felt her cares drifting away, and when Will said, 'That's another place we must visit while we're in Normandy; we'll have a whole day here when things at the hotel are not so pressing, shall we?' she smiled into his glittering dark eyes. She felt young and reckless and already half in love. 'I'd like that,' she agreed.

There was a long silence as they gazed into each other's eyes across the table, and Kate sucked in a small, unsteady breath.

At last he said softly, 'Your eyes are the colour of seaweed washed by the tide.'

She managed a shaky laugh. 'Very romantic! I thought you wrote tough mysteries, not love stories.'

'I can write a love story in my head, can't I? Nothing to stop a fellow from dreaming.' His voice dropped to a lower, thrilling tone. 'I'm in love with you, Kate. I can't forget it, and I don't want you to, either. Accepted, I can't do anything about it at the moment for various reasons, but I intend to keep the idea in your mind.'

Her eyes widened. 'You're serious, aren't you?'

'Dead serious,' he said. 'Never doubt it.'

She looked away, out of the window. He seemed to have a talent for reminding her. That was what *he* had said ten years ago: 'I love you. Never doubt it.'

She said in a cool little voice, 'I do doubt it. You've only known me two days.'

He said, 'Falling in love takes no time at all. It happens in a split second.'

'And falling out of love happens just as quickly, I suppose?' Her lip curled.

'I wouldn't know.' He looked straight into her eyes. 'You see, I've never been in love before.'

She laughed. 'Very funny!'

She dragged her gaze away from those liquid black eyes which seemed so honest. She said, with a little shiver, 'The sun has gone in—the cathedral looks quite different. Almost gloomy. I think we'd better be getting back to the hotel.'

Will sighed and signalled to the waiter.

'I think you should let me pay,' Kate said. 'You're supposed to be a visitor.'

He grinned, taking out his wallet. 'I'm the manager, have you forgotten?'

As they left the café Kate said rather crossly, 'It's all a huge joke to you, isn't it?'

He didn't reply to that question. He looked up at the cathedral. Now that the sun had gone the façade was bathed in faint, wispy mist. 'I see what they mean now,' Will said, 'when they say that it sometimes looks like a wedding cake. Rather appropriate, don't you agree?'

'I don't know what you're talking about,' Kate said. But she felt the colour rising into her cheeks.

'I think you do,' said Will. 'But, in case you don't, I'll explain that one day I intend to marry you, my beautiful Kate. And,' he added as they got into the car, 'I don't give up very easily.'

CHAPTER SIX

THERE was very little conversation on the drive back to the Ferme. The weather had changed completely and it was pouring with rain by now. The windscreen wipers on Becky's old car worked in a dot-and-carry-one fashion, and Will had to lean forward and concentrate on his driving. Kate, who was feeling anxious by this time about leaving the hotel unattended, went straight into the office when they arrived and switched on the answerphone. As she expected, the first message was in French, and she had to rewind the tape and wait for Will to join her.

When he came in he slumped into a chair. Kate eyed him worriedly. 'You're tired, aren't you? You shouldn't have been driving. Is your leg hurting?'

He waved away her solicitude. 'Don't fuss, Kate, I'm OK. I just need to stretch out, that's all. Was that a message I heard on the *répondeur*?'

She rewound the tape and switched it on. When the message came to an end he said, 'Turn it off a minute while I translate. It was from a firm in Caen. They're evidently booked to do some repairs to the roof here and they say they're coming to make a start tomorrow morning. Do you know anything about it?'

She shook her head, 'Becky didn't say anything about any builders. She must have forgotten.' She bit her lip. 'I wonder if we should put them off.'

'Better let them come and we can sort it out when they arrive, don't you think? If builders in Normandy are anything like builders in England one shouldn't let them get away once they appear. I'll deal with them if you like and find out what it's all about, OK?'

She nodded. 'You're probably right. Thank you. Let's see if there are any more messages and then I insist on your going and having a rest on your bed while I get us some supper. I can't have my right-hand man crocking up, you know,' she added with awful playfulness. Her feelings towards Will seemed to change erratically and at the moment she felt almost shy with him.

She pressed the switch hastily. The pips signalled another message. 'Hello, Katherine, dear. This is Edward. How are you getting along? Prepare yourself for a—I hope—pleasant surprise. I'm back in London.'

Out of the corner of her eye Kate saw that Will had got up and limped out of the room as Edward's precise voice droned on. 'My sister's baby arrived three weeks before expected and Mother has departed for Leicester to be with Marion. So that left me high and dry in Harrogate and I thought a nice way of filling in the remaining week of my holiday might be to spend it with you. How do you like the idea? I know you said the hotel is closed until Easter, and if your aunt can't put me up I could perhaps book in to another hotel and spend some of the time with you. I'd like to browse round Normandy—especially with you, Katherine. If I don't hear to the contrary from you I'll leave early tomorrow morning and be with you some time in the afternoon. I've got one or two rather important matters to talk over with you. I'll sign off now and take it that no news is good news. Goodbye, Katherine—or should I say *au revoir*?' Edward's self-conscious giggle ended the message.

Kate sat and stared at the instrument until the tape reached its end, with no more messages. She was still sitting there, frowning, when Will came back into the room. 'Finished?' he enquired. 'I trust you noticed my tact in removing myself.' He began searching through the papers on the desk. 'Now where is that letter from the building people? I've just remembered I saw one yesterday. Ah, here it is.'

Kate stared at him glassily. 'Edward says he's coming here tomorrow,' she said in a voice of doom.

'Don't you want to see him?' Will enquired mildly. 'I'd have thought——'

'I don't want him here,' she broke in impatiently. 'Can't you see it wouldn't do? If he found you here with me—alone—he might get the wrong idea. People have such one-track minds,' she added, giving him a rather nasty look.

He ignored the dig and said thoughtfully, 'If I could convince your aunt Becky that all was above-board, perhaps I can convince your nearly fiancé too. I don't mean I would go into the whole story,' he added hastily. 'I would have to revert to being the temporary manager. I could do that, I'm sure. It might be rather amusing.'

'It wouldn't be amusing for me,' Kate said coldly. 'There's only one way out. You'll have to leave first thing in the morning and find somewhere else to stay. Edward can't possibly be here until afternoon, so you'll have plenty of time.'

He leaned back against the desk, dark brows raised, a smug smile hovering around his mouth. 'And what about the builders? Will you be able to cope with them when they arrive? And phone calls when they crop up?'

Kate stamped her foot in frustration. 'Oh, it's all so stupid!'

'Worse things have happened,' he said placidly.

Kate's eyes sparkled with annoyance. 'I believe you want him to come. You'd enjoy play-acting, wouldn't you?'

'Don't let's quarrel,' he drawled. 'Why not get through to Edward and see if you can put him off until your aunt returns? You can make some excuse.'

'Some more "little white lies"?' Her lips curled. 'It seems to me that the more you insist on telling the truth, the more I'm pushed into concealing it.'

She shuffled some papers on the desk, not looking at him. 'I think it would be a good idea if you packed your bag. I'm not going to put Edward off.'

He gave her his pleading look—the one she'd given in to before. 'Are you determined? I'd rather like to stay and size up the opposition.'

'Don't be silly. Yes, I'm determined.'

'So,' Will said slowly, looking deep into her eyes, 'if you turn me out tomorrow morning we may never meet again.'

'I'm afraid not. I'm grateful for all you've done for me, but I think it had better end now.'

He watched her face for a long time, but she didn't allow her expression to soften.

'I see,' he said very quietly. Then he became very formal and businesslike. 'Will it be convenient if I use the computer while I have the chance? I've got very behind with my work.'

'Of course,' Kate said just as formally. 'I'm sorry to have taken up so much of your time today. You'll stop for some supper?'

'I'd rather go straight on, if you don't mind. I'll probably work very late.'

She nodded. 'I'll bring you some sandwiches and coffee, then.'

'That would be most kind,' said Will. He moved towards the computer and began to arrange notes and papers.

Kate went out to the kitchen. She felt a curious numb sensation in her chest. She assured herself she was doing the right thing. She would not risk losing Edward for a man like Will, charming and attractive—and irresponsible. All that business about intending to marry her! Quite absurd! It was about as true as the fiction he was so good at writing. He probably didn't know the difference between fact and fiction. No, she would never be so foolish as to get entangled with a man like Will Raven.

She would never let herself make the mistake poor Mother had made.

Squaring her slim shoulders, as she had so often seen Mother do, she turned her thoughts deliberately to Edward's arrival. They would eat in the dining-room when he was here, she planned. Edward liked things 'nice,' so meals in the kitchen were out. Kate took herself into the dining-room, which led through from the lounge, and set it to rights, turning back the chairs which Marie had stacked upside-down on the tables, dusting the massive sideboard, and removing imaginary crumbs from the carpet. After that she tidied up the lounge. She certainly wasn't going to light the log fire tonight. No more sitting in front of glowing logs—with Will. No, thank you! The electric heating was adequate, and Becky only kept the open fire in the lounge to give 'atmosphere' to the Ferme.

When everything was tidy, Kate went back to the kitchen and prepared two trays—one for herself and one for Will. She had been looking forward to cooking supper for them both, but if Will didn't want to join her for supper that was that. She wrenched off pieces of long baguette. It was rather stale by now—one bought bread fresh every day in France, she knew—but she couldn't help that. Will would have to put up with it. She washed salad and arranged it on the trays, with cheese, butter and fruit, and made coffee.

She carried one tray into the office and put it down beside Will on the littered desk. He lifted his head a fraction without taking his eyes from the screen. 'Thanks,' he said.

Kate went out and closed the door. She took her own tray into the lounge and turned on the television.

Doggedly she watched an old film which featured two men and three girls wandering around Paris. She couldn't understand a word they said, but it didn't seem to matter.

The hours crawled by. At nine o'clock she switched off the television and the lights and took her tray into the kitchen, pausing outside the office for a moment on her way. She heard the computer keys clicking away like mad. Will had forgotten everything but his work.

Kate suddenly felt dead tired. The rush of energy that had accompanied her resolution and decision had ebbed away.

Very slowly she went upstairs to bed.

Usually Kate wakened early and jumped out of bed, ready to face the day ahead. Next morning was quite different. Even a shower wasn't as refreshing as usual. She pulled on jeans and a sweater, brushed her hair, and padded downstairs to find that Will was there before her and was quietly eating the breakfast he had evidently prepared himself.

He looked up with a mock-wan smile. 'Good morning, Kate. As you can see, the condemned man is eating a hearty breakfast.'

'Good morning,' Kate said, turning her back as she went to the coffee machine. If he could go on joking then he couldn't be particularly upset at being turned out.

She carried a small, very strong cup of coffee and sat down opposite him.

He pushed plates across the table to her. 'Bread? Jam? Anything else?'

'Just coffee this morning,' she said. 'I'm not hungry.'

'Love taken your appetite away?'

'If you go on like this I shall scream,' Kate said between her teeth.

'Sorry. If I don't laugh I shall cry.' He wasn't laughing now.

'I know, I know, it's wretched of me to ask you to leave, after all you've done to help. Please do understand, Will.'

'OK,' he said. 'I'll go quietly.' He got up and carried his dishes to the sink. She watched him as he swilled them under the tap. He was wearing the black trousers and white shirt he had worn yesterday and his hair was carefully brushed. He was standing a little crookedly with his weight on the good leg. The sunshine touched the side of his neck, where the dark hair grew into it, giving it a bronze sheen. Kate wanted to get up and touch his neck, smooth his hair.

He turned to the door. 'I'll just finish packing up and then I'll see about finding a taxi. I should think Caen would be the nearest place to get one.'

'Where will you go?' Kate asked in a small voice.

He shrugged. 'The world is wide.'

He was going to disappear as he had appeared and she wasn't going to see him again. She didn't know where he lived; she didn't really know anything about him at all, except that he was a very successful writer who had injured himself in an encounter with a spider. He was going and she wouldn't ever see him again. She wanted to weep.

'I'll get my stuff from the office,' Will said. 'I'm sorry to part with the word processor; I was just getting really friendly with it. We worked very well together until about three o'clock this morning.'

'Oh, dear! You haven't had much sleep.' She hadn't had much sleep herself.

He smiled down at her—an oddly sweet smile. 'Dear little Kate,' he said softly. 'I'm going to miss you.'

She heard him go into the office and then the limping footsteps sounded as he made his way to the room at the end of the passage.

Kate sat at the table as if she were turned to stone. Was she doing something incredibly foolish? She buried her head in her hands to think, but nothing came.

Then the bell rang at the entrance door. The builders of course. She would have to try to deal with them herself. She crossed her fingers as she unlocked the heavy front door and swung it open.

A dark green Rover, which could only be Edward's was parked on the gravel outside. And, to her horror, standing at the front door, beaming, was Edward himself.

'Surprise, surprise!' cried Edward. 'Hello, Katherine. An early arrival—not too early, I trust.' He stepped inside the lounge, put both hands on her shoulders, and kissed her firmly and deliberately on the mouth, rather as if he had been rehearsing on the way here.

Kate swallowed hard. 'N-no, of course not.' Out of the corner of her eye she was aware of a shadowy form in the doorway leading from the adjoining dining-room into the side passage, and she raised her voice. 'How nice to see you, Edward! How did you manage to get here so soon? I didn't expect you until this afternoon. Do come in.'

The shadowy form melted away as she led Edward into the lounge. He looked very spruce this morning. His straight fair hair was brushed back carefully and his long, vaguely legal-looking face wore the pleased, happy expectant look of a little boy on his way to a party. He was wearing a charcoal-grey business suit with a pearl-grey shirt, whose sobriety was relieved by a red and white spotted tie. He placed his car coat neatly across the back of a chair before he sat down.

'Wonderful to see you, Katherine; I've looked forward to it. You got my message?'

'Yes,' she said. 'It was waiting for me last night when I got in from Rouen. I'd been there to visit my aunt in hospital. You don't know about all this, of course—I intended to write and tell you. Aunt Becky was ill when I arrived here and she had to go into hospital for an operation straight away.'

Edward clicked his tongue. 'What bad luck—so your holiday has been marred. You've been here on your own with just the servants—I gather that the hotel is closed.'

'It's a long story,' Kate said and added quickly, 'but you must let me look after you now you're here. Have you had breakfast?'

'Yes, thanks,' he said. 'I picked some food up as soon as the boat docked. You've probably gathered that I decided to come over by the night ferry. How is your aunt? I hope she's getting on satisfactorily.'

'Oh, yes, she's come through the operation very well.'

A noise outside made her get up to look through the window. A lorry was parked in front of the hotel and two workmen were getting out. 'Will you excuse me a moment, Edward?' she said. 'I'm expecting some builders and I'd better go and interview them.'

'Of course, dear.' Edward smiled pleasantly at her. 'Your aunt must be glad to have you here to watch her interests while she's away—you're such a capable girl.' He settled back in his chair as Kate made hastily for the front door.

The larger of the two men approached. 'Madame Arnot?'

'Er—no. *Non. Je suis* . . . Madame Arnot is ill—er—*malade.*' She groped helplessly for words.

Then she saw Will emerge round the corner of the building. He must have come through the back door. She beckoned to the man to come to meet him—well out of sight of the lounge window.

'Disaster!' she hissed. 'Edward's just arrived by the night ferry—and now these men are here. Will you cope with them?'

Will was grinning broadly. 'Mr Fixit will deal with the matter. You go back to Edward.'

'And what about you?' she groaned. 'What will you do?'

'Never mind me. Go on, out of the way, woman.'

Kate went back to Edward. Her palms were damp and a lock of richly red hair strayed down across her forehead.

She pushed it back. 'Well, at least let me make you some coffee now you've come all this way.'

'That would be delightful.' He looked around the lounge with its scrubbed wooden tables and massive sideboard. 'This is a funny old place,' he said. 'Very quaint—ye olde hostelry. They're very common in France, I believe.'

'Aunt Becky is very fond of it,' she told him coolly, leading the way into the kitchen. What was going on outside wouldn't be easily visible from here. Edward would have to drink his coffee in the kitchen.

While he drank his coffee Edward gave her a detailed account of his short stay in Harrogate, of the weather, the state of the roads, and his mother's sudden departure to his sister's bedside.

'And Mother phoned me later to say that Marion had had a little girl. Isn't that nice?'

Kate murmured what she hoped were the right words, while her brain was circling wildly round and round the fact that Will was just outside the back door. She could hear his voice, talking away in French to the builder.

'She wanted a girl so badly,' Edward went on, 'having two boys already. Just right, I think.' He smiled at Kate approvingly over the rim of his cup. 'You'd make a beautiful mother, Katherine,' he said.

'Oh,' Kate murmured. 'Oh, thank you, Edward. But not for some time yet, I think.'

A slight frown creased his smooth forehead. 'You're not saying that you don't want a family, surely?'

'One of these days I expect I will.' It occurred to her that Edward was making sure of his ground in advance

and she knew quite suddenly that if—when—he pro-
posed marriage she was going to refuse. 'What are they
going to call the little girl?' she went on hastily.

'They can't decide. They think——'

A brisk tap on the outside door and Will walked in.
Kate's eyes widened in horror. Now what?

He stood very straight and formal. He gave a small
deferential bow. 'May I 'ave your attention, if you please,
mademoiselle. Ze men from ze builders wish to speak
with you *un moment*.'

Kate choked back a wild laugh. She pushed back her
chair, looking helplessly from one man to the other.
'Edward, this is Monsieur...' She pulled a horrible face
at Will behind Edward's back. 'I'm sorry—I didn't catch
your name when you arrived.'

Will bowed again. 'Le Corbeau, Guillaume le
Corbeau—at your service, *mademoiselle, monsieur*.' He
bowed again and went out.

Kate got to her feet hastily. 'Won't be a moment. Just
have to sort out the builders,' she murmured, and followed Will into the yard, banging the door behind her.

Will was waiting for her outside the door, the builder's
men hovering in the background. 'Very funny,' Kate said
bitterly. 'Now we *are* in a muddle, aren't we?'

'Why?' Will was at his most bland. 'I thought I was
pretty convincing. After all, I *am* half-French—and I
only spoke the truth.' He gave her a mocking smile. 'It
was you, my honest little darling, who pulled the wool
over Edward's eyes. For Little Miss Georgie Washington,
who never tells a lie, I thought you managed quite well.'

'That's right, gloat,' she spat at him like an angry
kitten. 'I'm quite well aware that you're having a bad
influence on me. And what's the Monsieur Corbeau idea,
anyway?'

'*Corbeau* is French for raven. Clever, don't you think?
I thought it would be more convincing if I were all
French, instead of just half.'

She let that pass. 'What about these builder people?'

'They say they've got instructions from your aunt to mend a small hole in the roof—up there.' He indicated the place. 'Shall I tell them to get on with it?'

'Yes, I suppose so.' She was simmering with temper by now. 'Well, you'd better get back to your office— Monsieur le Corbeau—and stay there. You'll be able to finish your book. Just keep out of our way, that's all.'

He gave her his little deferential bow. 'Certainly *mademoiselle*. Your wish is my command.'

'Oh, you—you...' Words failed her and she flounced back into the kitchen.

Edward stood up politely. 'All fixed up? Can't the manager fellow see to the matter for you?' He frowned. 'I'm not sure I like the look of him, Katherine. Is he OK, do you think?'

Kate sat down. She was feeling rather weak. 'The manager, do you mean? He works for a friend of my aunt's so I'm sure he must be trustworthy.'

Edward was still frowning. 'Katherine, dear, I'm not sure I approve of the set-up here, you know. How long has he been here?'

'W—Monsieur le Corbeau? Oh, a couple of days.'

Edward's fair brows rose. He looked positively outraged. 'You mean he's sleeping here?'

'Yes, of course,' Kate said, trying not to sound defensive.

'Oh, well, I suppose there are servants here too, so you're not alone.'

'The servants are on holiday at present,' Kate announced. 'But——'

'You mean...you've been here alone—with that fellow?'

Kate laughed merrily. 'Oh, Edward, you sound like a Victorian papa. I assure you that he's perfectly harmless.'

'I'm not at all convinced of that,' Edward said darkly. 'But I suppose it doesn't matter because I shall be here, and I shall stay until your aunt returns. When are you expecting her back?'

'I don't really know,' Kate said vaguely. 'It might be a couple of weeks. She had her operation only the day before yesterday.'

'Look, Katherine.' Edward drew himself up to his full height. 'I will not have you staying here alone with that man after I have to return to London. We must make other arrangements.'

Kate got to her feet. 'I certainly won't leave the hotel until Aunt Becky comes back,' she said. 'And, really, Edward, I won't be ordered about, you know.'

For a moment they glared at each other. Then Edward relaxed and took one of her hands in both of his. 'Oh, Katherine, don't let's quarrel when I've just arrived. I'm not trying to order you about—it's just that I—I care about you. I've looked forward so much to having this time with you. Let's leave it for the moment, shall we? Now, what are we going to do today—shall we make some plans?'

'I'll go and prepare your room first,' she said, edging towards the door. 'You go and make yourself comfortable in the lounge and when I come down we can talk.' Thankfully she escaped upstairs.

She chose the room at the end of the first-floor passage—the one furthest away from her own room. Not that she suspected Edward of having any plans to seduce her, but rather because she thought it would appeal to his sense of propriety, after his outburst about Will.

She had dark thoughts about Will as she made up the bed. Ever since Will turned up she had found herself behaving in a despicable fashion. True, it was because the truth, spoken baldly, would have hurt other people— first Aunt Becky and now Edward. Edward was rather sweet; he really had been concerned for her safety and if that made him sound a little pompous—well, that was just Edward's way and she could forgive him. Perhaps it was a bit old-fashioned of her, but she found that she liked a man to be protective. She was sure now that he intended to ask her to marry him. That remark about wanting to have children, and the way he'd looked at her, proved it. Edward would be a good father, she thought, plumping up the pillows. Perhaps a rather too firm disciplinarian, but that might be no bad thing these days. He was honest and affectionate and reliable. Oh, yes, he would make a good husband and father.

She heard his step on the landing and went to the door.

'I've brought my bag up,' Edward said. 'Is this my room? It's delightfully French, isn't it? All the heavy dark furniture and the bric-à-brac on the walls!' He gestured to the water-colours painted by Becky's late husband, to the gilt-framed mirrors and the pink-shaded lights.

Kate suppressed a twinge of irritation. Edward didn't mean to sound critical, she was sure.

He prodded the bed, as no doubt his mother had taught him to do in hotels. 'Looks very comfy. Perhaps I'll have a kip until lunch if that's OK by you.' He stretched out on the bed and said with an embarrassed little giggle, 'You wouldn't care to join me, Katherine?'

Kate stared. 'What exactly do you mean?'

He flushed. 'Have I spoken out of turn? I've always understood that a trial run is usual and advisable.'

Laughter was Kate's only refuge and she laughed heartily. 'This is so sudden. Isn't that the usual thing to say? No, thanks, I'll deny myself the pleasure. You have a nice sleep and come down when you're ready for lunch—about half-past twelve.'

She was still chuckling at the flabbergasted look on Edward's face when she got downstairs. Dear Edward, he was so very shy and so very anxious to do the right thing. Perhaps that was no bad quality in a man, she thought. He would soon lose his shyness when—if—they were married. Feeling domesticated, she took Becky's straw carrier down from its hook and set off for the village.

The sun was shining and the countryside was green and sparkling after yesterday's rain. Kate felt her spirits improving with the weather. In the village she bought bread at the bakery, cheese and salad at the little village shop, and—after some difficulty—managed to get a can of milk, promising to return the can. The dairyman seemed to understand her very broken French—or perhaps it was her smile that did the trick.

She lingered on the way back to the hotel. After all the hassle she was beginning to feel that she was on holiday at last. She hummed a little tune as she strolled along the lane. Perhaps things weren't so bad after all. Surely Will would have the decency to keep to himself, and she would take Edward on some sightseeing expeditions, and by the time he left they *might*—just *might*—be engaged, which would alter the situation entirely.

The hotel came in sight, nestling among its surrounding trees. Long and low and cosy-looking, it seemed to breathe, 'Welcome'. She didn't wonder that Becky loved it.

As she grew nearer she saw the tall ladder that leant against the gables of the roof. Right up at the top of the ladder was a blob of scarlet. Kate drew nearer—it was a man in a scarlet jacket.

Her heart gave a huge thump. Will—up there at the top of the ladder. Will, who had only just begun to recover from a bad fall. What on earth . . . ?

She began to hurry. Then at the entrance she came to a dead halt, transfixed by terror. The ladder was wobbling horribly.

As it lurched sideways she heard herself scream, 'Will—Will.' And then she was tearing across the gravel to where the fallen ladder lay—and by its side a horribly inert man's form in a scarlet wind-cheater.

Relax with **FOUR FREE** Temptations

PLUS A FREE CUDDLY TEDDY AND SPECIAL MYSTERY GIFT.

plus two FREE gifts!

Temptations offer you all the age-old passion and tenderness of romance, now experienced through very contemporary relationships. And to introduce to you this powerful and highly charged series, we'll send you **four Temptations plus two FREE gifts** when you complete and return this card. We'll also reserve you a subscription to Reader Service which means you could enjoy:

■ **FOUR BRAND NEW NOVELS** sent direct to you each month.

■ **FREE POSTAGE AND PACKING** we pay all the extras.

■ **FREE MONTHLY NEWSLETTER** packed with special offers, competitions, author news and much more.

■ **HELPFUL FRIENDLY SERVICE** telephone our Customer Care team on 081-684 2141

Turn over to claim your FREE Temptations and FREE gifts.

FREE books and gifts claim

Yes! Please send me four Temptations and two FREE gifts without obligation. Please also reserve me a subscription to Reader Service; which means that I can look forward to four brand new Temptations for just £7.40 each month (subject to VAT). Postage and packing is FREE. If I decide not to subscribe I will write to you within 10 days. Any free books and gifts will remain mine to keep. I understand that I may cancel or suspend my subscription at any time. I am over 18 years of age.

7A3T

Ms/Mrs/Miss/Mr _____

Address _____

_____

_____ Postcode _____

Signature _____

Mills & Boon
Reader Service
FREEPOST
P.O. Box 236
Croydon
CR9 9EL

CHAPTER SEVEN

KATE was about a hundred yards away from the house. She dropped her basket, and the can of milk spilled its contents over the road. She was only dimly aware of footsteps following her as she tore across the gravel towards the prostrate form in the red anorak.

He was lying on his side with one leg stuck out awkwardly, his face half buried in the black earth of the flower-bed.

Kate went down on her knees beside him. 'Will—Will, darling...darling...' She put one hand very gently under the dark, matted hair and turned away for a moment, not daring to look down. When she nerved herself to do so she could hardly believe what she saw. The eyes were closed. The face, spattered with damp earth, was that of a very young man—and it was not Will's face.

At that moment the running footsteps stopped and a strong hand pulled her to her feet. 'Let me look,' said Will.

Kate's brain seemed to go into neutral after that. She saw Will kneeling beside the injured boy, heard the rapid exchange between Will and the other builders' man, and couldn't understand a word, of course.

At last Will got to his feet and limped rapidly into the hotel. Kate stared at the builders' man as he began to rattle away to her in French and she shook her head. '*Je ne comprends pas*,' she murmured weakly.

Her legs felt like jelly, but she forced them to follow Will into the hotel and to the office, where he was thumbing through a directory.

'An ambulance,' he muttered. 'I don't know where—ah, here it is.'

He spoke urgently into the phone. When he put down the instrument he said tersely, 'Kate, will you go into my room and get the duvet from there? We mustn't move him.'

She nodded and did what she was told. Outside again, she and Will covered the unconscious boy. He looked so young, too frail to be doing a tough building job.

'Is it—is it bad?' she whispered to Will.

He shook his head. 'No way of knowing,' he said. 'At least he's alive.'

Kate knelt beside the boy, talking to him softly, as if he could hear and understand. 'It won't be long,' she whispered. 'Hang on, they'll soon be here and then it'll be all right.'

Suddenly the long dark lashes fluttered and the boy moaned faintly.

Kate looked up at Will, her eyes shining. 'He's conscious,' she said.

He nodded without speaking. His face was grim, serious. She'd never seen him look like that.

'The ambulance shouldn't be long,' he said.

At last a small ambulance drove up and the business of getting the boy on to a stretcher and installed in the van began. Kate walked beside the stretcher, talking softly to the boy all the time. Under the blanket the ambulance men had laid over him, her hand touched his cold one. 'Don't give up,' she whispered again. 'You're going to be all right.'

The stretcher slid into the van, one man jumped in beside it, and it was gone.

Reaction struck Kate. Thick tears gathered in her eyes and she began to sob like a little girl. She felt Will's arms go round her, holding her tightly against his warm body, and it was infinitely comforting. She pressed against him,

needing him—loving the closeness of the contact between them.

Then he wasn't holding her any longer. She wiped her
eyes with the back of her hand and frowned up at him,
then turned her head to see Edward standing in front of
them, his face a cold, angry mask.

'What exactly does this mean?' he demanded icily.

Will gave him an insolent look. 'Do not disturb
yourself, *monsieur*,' he said smoothly, handing Kate over
to Edward as if she were a parcel to be delivered.
'*Mademoiselle* 'as been upset and I 'ave comforted her,
that is all.'

'Oh, yes?' Edward sneered.

Will waved a hand. 'Merely in a—'ow do you say?—
in a brotherly fashion,' he said. And, turning round, he
limped away quickly, the builders' man at his heels.

Kate staggered into the lounge and collapsed into a
chair, Edward following.

'I don't understand.' He took a chair opposite. 'What
upset you? That man—he didn't...?'

'Of course not,' Kate told him wearily. 'You missed
it all. A ladder slipped and one of the builders was badly
injured. They've only just got him away by ambulance.
It—it was horrid.'

'Ah, forgive me, I didn't understand,' Edward said,
his face clearing. 'The injured man—was he killed?'

'He was alive,' Kate said. 'I don't know how badly
injured he is.'

Edward pursed his lips. 'I hope he was fully insured,'
he said. 'Otherwise your aunt might find herself liable
to meet a large claim.'

For moments Kate stared at him speechlessly. There
was a decided chill in her voice as she said, 'I must go
and see to the lunch now, Edward. Can you amuse
yourself for an hour or so?'

Edward didn't notice the chill, or if he did he ignored it. He expressed himself quite happy to put in an hour on some work he'd brought with him.

'And after lunch,' he went on, 'shall we go out for a run in my car? There doesn't seem much opportunity for conversation here and there's something I particularly want to say to you.' He smiled mysteriously. 'You may be surprised, but I think you'll be quite pleased.'

When Edward had gone upstairs to his room Kate went out and retrieved the basket she had dropped. The milk was nearly all gone, but she carried what remained of her shopping expedition into the kitchen and prepared to make a vegetable soup for lunch, her thoughts on Edward's last remark. Pleased? I wonder if I will be pleased, she thought as she chopped carrots absently.

She couldn't get the face of that boy out of her mind. 'Oh, let him be all right; he's so young,' she whispered.

Will put his head round the door and walked into the kitchen. 'All alone? Cleared up the little misunderstanding, I hope.' He didn't wait for her answer. His face was very grave as he went on, 'That was a nasty do, wasn't it? God, it was a shock. I was sure one of them had killed himself when I heard the crash.'

Kate nodded dumbly, her head lowered over the chopping-board. She heard Will come up behind her and a shiver ran through her body.

He tipped up her chin and looked into her face. 'Are you OK? You're making heavy weather of those carrots. Here, let me help.' He took the knife out of her hand and began chopping the carrots expertly, talking away as he did so. 'I got the number of the hospital they were taking the boy to,' he said. 'We'll be able to ring up and enquire how he's doing. The ambulance seemed well-equipped—oxygen laid on. He should have every chance.'

Kate had stepped aside and her eyes were fixed on his hands as he finished the carrots and started to peel the onions she'd put out. She was beginning to realise how many sides there were to Will Raven. His hands were so strong, the fingers so deft.

He turned his head. 'Mind you don't start weeping again.' Then the knife dropped from his hand and he looked deep into her eyes. 'You called me "darling",' he said slowly. '"Will, darling"—that's what you said.'

'I thought you'd been killed,' Kate said in a choky little voice.

They stared at each other for what seemed minutes and neither of them could look away. Then Kate pulled out a hanky. 'It's the onions,' she said, trying to smile and failing miserably.

She blew her nose and wiped her eyes. 'Why was the boy wearing your red anorak? It was yours, wasn't it?'

'I made him put it on. The kid wasn't well; he was shivering. I told his mate—the older man—that he'd better send the boy home, but he didn't want to know. Probably didn't want to tackle the job on his own. He's scared stiff now—thinks he'll be blamed for what happened. Quite right, too, he should never have let the kid go up that ladder without checking that it was safe. Apparently the woodwork of the eaves was rotten and the extra weight caused it to break. I'd like to strangle the fellow in charge.' He looked fierce, contemptuous.

A little shiver ran through Kate. I wouldn't like him to look at me like that, she thought. She changed the subject quickly. 'Let me finish the vegetables; I'm OK now.' She drew in a breath and added, 'Edward and I are going out for a drive after lunch.'

There was a heavy silence. Will washed his hands and dried them carefully. 'I'll come out and help myself when I'm ready,' he said. 'You'll be serving Edward his lunch in the dining-room, I expect?'

Kate nodded. 'I thought it would be——'

Will held up a hand. 'Never apologise, never explain,' he said wryly. 'I know the score.' He limped out of the kitchen and she heard the study door close behind him.

Kate's technical training had built in her the ability to
concentrate and now she concentrated like mad—on
making the soup. When that was simmering away she
unpacked Becky's shopping basket and rescued from it
everything that hadn't been soaked in milk when she had
dropped the basket in the lane. She found a freshly laun-
dered red and white check cloth and spread it on one of
the small tables in the dining-room, picked some blue-
bells in the back garden and arranged them in one of
Becky's Wedgwood vases. Then she looked around to
find something else to do that would take her mind off
the problem that she was going to have to face eventually.
The massive old sideboard provided the answer. Marie
kept it beautifully, of course, but it wouldn't do it any
harm to be polished all over again. Kate found that polishing was soothing to the nerves and, by the time it was
finished to her satisfaction, the table set, and the soup
poured into a tureen and brought to the table, Kate found
that she felt reasonably capable of dealing with Edward,
and the mysterious thing he had to say to her—which,
she was fairly sure, wasn't very mysterious at all.

She went up to the room at the end of the passage
and knocked on the door. 'Lunch is ready,' she called
out. Edward appeared immediately, rubbing his hands
and declaring himself extremely hungry.

He was delighted with everything—the arrangement
of the table, the flowers, the food, the wine. 'You made
the soup yourself, Katherine? I must congratulate you.'

She felt as if she'd passed some important examin-
ation with flying colours. Edward's mother would no
doubt subject her to the same kind of test in due course.
Why did she have to think of that? It was silly and petty.
His mother was probably a charming, friendly woman.
'Thank you, Edward, I'm glad you're satisfied.'

He wrinkled his brow at that. 'Satisfied? What do you
mean, Katherine?'

She coughed. 'I mean, I'm glad you're pleased,' she said hastily, and watched his face clear. He couldn't help expressing himself rather formally, she supposed. It was probably his legal training. When she went into the kitchen to make coffee she encountered Will, helping himself liberally to soup.

'Jolly good stuff, this,' he said. He glanced towards the dining-room, and lowered his tone to a conspiratorial whisper. 'How's it going, Kate?'

She tried to freeze him with a glance. 'I'm having a civilised lunch for once,' she said, and could have kicked herself as she remembered that Will had given her lunch in Rouen yesterday and how they had enjoyed looking at the cathedral together. 'I mean . . .' she began.

But Will had disappeared into the office with his bowl of soup.

In the lounge she put the coffee tray on a small table before the log fire, which she had lit earlier.

'Very cosy!' Edward seemed to have mellowed since he saw the hotel this morning. Perhaps he'd been hungry.

He talked about Harrogate, and how he was looking for a small house to buy there. 'It would be most—er—pleasurable to be near Mother, and to drive up there at weekends. The London flat is inclined to be somewhat cramped. I've got my eye on a small house—quite old and interesting—and it's for offer at a reasonable price. I'd like to take you up to have a look at it some time—you could advise me.' He giggled. 'A woman's touch, you know.'

When she didn't reply he put down his cup and looked keenly into her face. 'What's the matter, Katherine? You weren't listening.'

She said, 'I'm sorry, Edward. I can't help thinking about that poor boy who had the accident and wondering how he is.'

He squeezed her hand. 'You're a dear, caring girl, Katherine, but you mustn't take on other people's troubles, you know. I'm sure the boy will survive. Young bones, and all that. Did you hear what I was saying?'

She blinked at him. 'About the house in Harrogate? Yes, I heard. I think it would be a very good idea, Edward. And now, will you excuse me? I have a few things to see to in the kitchen.'

He stood up politely. 'Certainly. And when you're ready, may we go out for our drive? I took the precaution of bringing a Normandy guidebook with me, so I'll be planning out an itinerary.'

Kate cleared the table in the dining-room, washed the dishes, and left the kitchen tidy. Then she opened the office door.

Will was working at the computer. Her eyes fixed themselves on the back of his head; there was something about the way his hair grew into his neck . . . Oh, stop it, Kate, she told herself. She said, 'Edward and I are going out for a drive. Do you mind holding the fort here? And get yourself something to eat—you know where everything is.' She hesitated, biting her lip. 'I feel bad about asking you.'

'It's OK,' he said briefly, turning back to the screen. 'Have a good time.'

When she had closed the door Kate waited for a moment uncertainly, her hand on the knob. She had an urge to go back and somehow put things right with Will. It had been so easy to talk to Will and now it wasn't easy any longer. They weren't communicating. But she didn't know what to say so she sighed and walked up the back stairs to her room.

Here she brushed her heavy red hair into a shining coil on the top of her head, smoothed on lipstick that blended with her coffee-coloured jersey dress, picked up her short white coat and handbag and went back into the lounge.

Edward smiled approvingly. 'You look very nice, Katherine. It's such a delight, in these days, to see a woman look—well, refined.'

'Thank you,' Kate said.

Driving with Edward in his glossy new Rover was quite a change from driving in Becky's five-year-old Renault—with Will.

Edward was very proud of his new car and enthused about all the new technology. Kate sank back into the luxury of soft leather and made the right noises in response. When Edward came to the end of the list she said, 'Where are we going?'

'I've got a treat for you—I hope,' said Edward. 'I see from the guidebook that a wonderful place to visit is the famous Monet gardens at Giverny. Apparently there was a famous French artist called Monet who presented these gardens to the nation. Would you like to go there, Katherine?'

Kate's heart sank. Will had talked about taking her to the Monet gardens and she wanted to see them with him—and nobody else. She wanted to walk with him through the flowers, to see the way his black eyes glinted into hers, to thrill to the touch of his hand on her arm. She closed her eyes. This feeling for Will had nothing to do with the good, solid marriage that she was sure that Edward was going to suggest.

She wanted marriage. Now that Mother had gone she wanted to make a life of her own that was more than just a career—however interesting. She wanted a home, children. The thought of boys with Will's black hair and impish grin made her feel weak—but Will wasn't the marrying kind, however much he pretended to be serious about her.

However unreasonable it was, she knew that she didn't want to go to the Monet gardens with Edward.

'I think the gardens might be rather disappointing at this time of the year,' she said. 'The countryside really isn't at its best yet. How about going to Caen? There must be something to see there—museums and old churches and so on.'

'Yes, that sounds a better idea.' She thought Edward seemed relieved. She guessed that he would be more at home in a town setting than a country one.

They drove to Caen and walked round the city, most of whose buildings, Edward read out from his guidebook, had been flattened during the fighting that followed the Allied landings on the Normandy beaches in 1944. Edward was full of praise for the way the city had been restored. Kate was, too; she just wished that he would stop reading reams from his guidebook. She suggested they might find a café and have tea. That was a mistake, for Edward reminded her gently that tea wasn't looked upon as the national beverage it was in England, and even if they could obtain it it would probably not be up to standard.

'Let's try it, all the same,' said Kate, who was longing for a cup of tea.

The tea, when it arrived after a long wait, was definitely not to Edward's liking, and he would have remonstrated with the proprietress if Kate, wincing at the thought of Edward using his creaky French to start a scene, hadn't stopped him.

A clock was striking five somewhere when they came out of the café. Edward got out his guidebook again. 'We'll see if there are any good hotels where we can get a meal a little later,' he said, as they walked along by the river.

Kate drew her white jacket closer. 'It's getting rather cold, and we'd have time to put in,' she said. 'Let's go back to the hotel and I'll cook something.'

'I'd like to take you out to dinner,' Edward insisted. 'I've been looking forward to it. We'll go back to the car and have a nice drive around the district. The car heater's really excellent. You'll soon warm up.'

They trudged back to the car and Edward arranged a rug solicitously over Kate's knees. 'There! Now, let's have a little tour.'

They drove and drove. Miles and miles of fields. Fields and trees. More fields. Cows.

Edward discoursed on the dairy farming of Normandy. He'd evidently been mugging it up in his guidebook. Kate said, 'Yes, how interesting!' and her thoughts ranged from Becky, to Will, to the injured boy in hospital and back again. She couldn't expect Edward to be interested in her worries, she told herself, and she guessed that he would have a brisk way of dealing with worries if she tried to talk about them.

At last it began to get dark and Edward steered the car on to the motorway. 'We're only about five kilometres from a village called Beuvron-en-Auge, which is supposed to be one of the most beautiful villages in France, and it's possible to dine well there. I think we'll try it.'

By now Kate was beyond caring. 'Very well, Edward,' she said listlessly.

He looked keenly at her. 'What's the matter, Katherine?' Edward said sharply. Everything's the matter, she thought, and said, 'I'm OK, just a bit tired.'

'Cheer up, we'll soon be there.' He sounded faintly irritable now, but when, shortly afterwards, he drove the car on to the forecourt of an inn of some sort, his spirits revived.

He led the way inside, settled Kate by the fire, and ordered drinks. 'A small whisky for you, Katherine, as you're cold and tired.'

Kate didn't say she hated whisky. Edward was doing his best to be a good host. She sipped the drink and felt a little better, while Edward went away to enquire about a meal.

He returned to say that they would serve dinner immediately, although it was earlier than usual, and a waiter appeared, to lead them into a completely empty dining-room.

Edward consulted the menu card. 'Apparently the specialty here is a tripe dish,' he said in delight. 'Sounds perfectly splendid. I'm from the north of England, you know, and tripe is just the job for me. How about you?'

'I'll try anything once,' Kate agreed. 'I've never had tripe.'

'You'll love it,' Edward insisted, but she doubted if she would. This was turning out to be the most disastrous outing of her life. It couldn't get much worse. In this she was mistaken.

It was after dinner when Edward dropped his bombshell. They were drinking coffee in the lounge, sitting one each end of a comfortable sofa near the fire.

'This is cosy, isn't it?' Edward said, looking around. 'We've got the place almost to ourselves—we won't be interrupted.' He cleared his throat. 'There are a couple of important things I want to talk to you about, Katherine. I didn't spring them on you sooner because I wasn't sure how you'd feel and whether you'd be pleased or not. I remembered that when we first met you told me you hadn't had any contact with your father for many years, and didn't wish to have anything to do with him again. I think that was how you put it.'

Kate gulped scalding hot coffee from the tiny cup, and put it down with a clatter. She said coldly, 'I haven't changed my mind, Edward, if you're thinking of trying to communicate with him. And I don't wish to talk about it.'

'I'm afraid we must, dear,' he said gently. 'You see, your father has been to see me, and I've had a long talk with him.'

'*What*?' Kate shouted.

'Ssh!' Edward touched her hand, glancing nervously round the empty room. He went on rapidly, 'He was, of course, notified of your mother's death.'

'Oh!' She looked at him blankly. 'I'd no idea your firm was still in touch.'

'Apparently that is the case. I've been going through Mr Grayson's books and papers—you know that our principal, Mr Grayson, had to give up suddenly through ill health. I'm afraid his work was—er—slightly disorganised, but when your mother died I found your father's address and wrote to him to apprise him of the fact.'

'Why did you do that? I shouldn't have thought it was necessary.' Kate stuck out her chin aggressively.

Edward eyed her with a shrewd gleam. 'Look, Katherine, dear, you really mustn't be so bitter about it. Divorce happens, you know, and if two people don't get on it's better that they should part. We see it all the time in our profession.'

'I bet you do,' Kate said.

He ignored that and went on, 'Your father very much wants to see you, Katherine. I told him I would have to get your permission to—er—divulge your whereabouts so that I could put him in touch with you. And I thought it would be a good idea to come out and see you. Which,' he added with a knowing little smile, 'I wanted to do very much.'

'Well, if you've come to persuade me to see him I'm afraid you've wasted your time,' Kate said. Under the table her knees were beginning to shake. 'And I don't want to talk about it.'

But Edward hadn't given up yet. 'I think that perhaps you should see your father, Katherine. Have a talk with him. He impressed me very favourably. He seems to be a highly successful man.'

Kate's lips curled. 'You mean you think I might be missing out on a good thing.'

Edward looked hurt. 'You needn't put it quite so—er—straightforwardly, Katherine.'

'I'm a straightforward person,' she said. 'But don't you really mean "crudely"?'

He fidgeted with his lapel. 'This confrontational attitude isn't like you, Katherine. I hardly seem to recognise you.'

Edward's face had gone very white. She felt almost sorry for him. 'No,' she said, 'but then I don't think you have ever known me very well, Edward.'

And that, she thought, was that. End of a beautiful romance. Except that it never had been a romance. She couldn't imagine Edward telling her that her eyes were the colour of seaweed. He probably didn't know what colour her eyes were.

The drive back to the hotel was accomplished in silence. When he had stopped the car Edward took one of Kate's cold hand in his. 'I'm sorry that this has upset you, my dear. I wouldn't want to do that, but I had to tell you. Are you angry with me?'

Just hold on to your patience a bit longer, Kate, she instructed herself. She didn't feel angry any more; she just wanted to get away by herself.

'Of course you had to tell me,' she said. 'It's your job. How could I hold it against you?'

He said eagerly, 'Then I haven't spoilt my chance with you, Katherine? I've thought so much about you. I hoped we might—— '

'Please!' She removed her hand from his. 'I think it would be better if we kept our relationship on a purely professional basis in future, Edward.' Heavens! she thought, I'm beginning to talk like him now.

There was a lengthy silence. Then Edward sighed deeply. 'I see,' he said at last. 'Well, then, I suppose that is that.'

Poor Edward—she had hurt him, hurt his pride. But she couldn't possibly...

'Thank you,' she said. '"Just good friends", that's what they say, isn't it?'

He got out and opened the car door for her. He didn't even refer to the central-locking device on his new car. 'I hope so,' he said.

Once in the hotel Edward became his usual organised self. 'I'll go up and pack now. I'd like to leave very early in the morning—soon after five o'clock. Don't trouble about breakfast for me—I'll have something on the ferry. We'll say *au revoir* now, shall we? I'll be in touch with you later, when your mother's affairs are finalised.'

He held out a hand and Kate put hers into it. '*Au revoir*, Edward,' she said warmly. 'And thank you for your help.' She hesitated. 'I definitely don't wish to have anything to do with my—my father ever again, and you may explain that to him in any way you think best.'

A very faint smile touched his mouth. 'My client's wishes are my commands,' he said, and walked to the stairs. Halfway up he paused and looked down again, half hopefully, as though she might have changed her mind. Then he went slowly upwards again.

She stood looking after him. Perhaps, after all, Edward did have a sense of humour.

He really was a good man, she reminded herself, thinking that when she came here, only three days ago, she had been on the point of accepting him as her future husband.

But that was before things happened. Before...

She turned to go into the kitchen and saw Will standing in the dining-room doorway, his hands stuck in his pockets, a very curious expression on his face.

The world suddenly began to turn upside-down, stopped, turned back again, as she stood staring at him. She stood frozen by the impact of the devastating new thing that had happened to her. For the first time in her life, she was in love.

She was in love with Will Raven.

CHAPTER EIGHT

'HELLO, Kate,' said Will, with a glance at the departing form of Edward. 'I hope I haven't butted in.'

Kate put her hand on the arm of a chair to steady herself. The room seemed to be revolving slowly before her eyes.

'N-no,' she stammered. So this was what it was like to fall in love—this overwhelming consciousness of the other person! The room stopped revolving and came to rest.

There was nobody there but Will—nobody in the whole world. He hadn't shaved and there was a dark shadow on his chin; his hair was mussed up; his white shirt was hanging open almost to the waist. He looked wonderful—fabulous, she thought besottedly.

He gave her a curious glance, not quite meeting her eyes. 'Had a good time?'

'Er—yes, thank you.'

'You were well out of it,' he said. 'All hell's been let loose here. We've had the director of the building company, breathing fire. Also the police.'

Kate put a hand to her mouth. 'Oh, Will, and I wasn't here to help you to cope with them.'

'I coped,' he said briefly. 'There wasn't much you could have done. They were extremely talkative.'

She tried not to think he meant that as a put-down. 'All the same, I feel awful about leaving you. I wouldn't have done if....' She bit her knuckle unhappily.

'OK, I know the score. It doesn't matter.' He sounded as if he couldn't care less how she felt.

She said, 'Have you heard any more about the boy? We were going to telephone the hospital.'

'I rang a few minutes ago. He's holding his own. That's about all they would say, except that he's got a double fracture of one leg and is covered in scratches and bruises. I've been out with the building fellow to look at the place where it happened, and we think the holly bush under the window must have broken his fall—probably saved his life. We have to wait until morning to hear any more.'

She nodded slowly. 'Thank you, Will. You've been marvellous—I don't know what I should have done without you. But I've said that before, haven't I?' She heard herself laugh stupidly.

He merely shrugged and turned towards the office.

She couldn't let him go like this. She ran after him, tripped over a corner of the rug, and lurched sideways against his arm. For a blissful moment she was held close to him. She could feel the steady thump of his heart. Then he put her away. 'Steady on, Kate,' he said casually. 'We don't want any more accidents.'

He went back into the office and closed the door without any word. He didn't even say goodnight.

Kate felt as if a chill wind had blown over her. For a moment she stood looking at the closed door, but hadn't the courage to open it. She couldn't possibly go to bed and lie awake and she did the only thing that occurred to her—she went into the kitchen and put the kettle on for tea. When it was made she stood looking down at Becky's favourite brown teapot, her heart beating erratically. Should she risk it or not?

She crossed the passage and opened the office door a crack. 'Will...?'

'Yes?' he said shortly over his shoulder.

Kate wasn't used to feeling nervous about approaching a man. In her job she had to do it all the time. But this was different.

She said through dry lips, 'I've made some tea. I wondered if you'd like a cup—to help you with your labours,' she added.

'I don't think so, thanks.' He continued to peer at the computer screen.

'Oh.' She stood looking helplessly at his averted head.

'Aren't you sharing it with your nearly fiancé?' he said absently.

She came a little further into the room, her heart still thumping.

'He's not...' she began, and stopped. She didn't think he was listening. And what did she say? It's all over between Edward and me. I'm free now, if you still want me? No, she wouldn't sink as low as that. She ignored the question, murmured, 'Goodnight,' and left him to his writing.

Back in the kitchen she drank a solitary cup of tea and then went up to bed, niggled by a horrid feeling of anticlimax and on the verge of tears.

She swilled her face in cold water and blew her nose. She must be sensible, she told herself, as she got into bed. What had happened to the cool, self-collected young career woman who had arrived here only a few days ago, with the intention of making up her mind about Edward? She wasn't going to turn one man down only to begin mooning over another, who was obviously more interested in his work than in her. She would go to sleep and not give him another thought.

Sleep, however, refused to come. She lay awake, wrapped in dreamy imaginings of Will and herself—mostly erotic—until she had to get up and walk around the room to calm herself down. Eventually she fell into such a deep sleep that she didn't hear Edward's car starting below the window. But when she looked out of the window next morning it had gone.

Will was nowhere to be seen when she got downstairs. She'd had a sketchy breakfast and was planning her

shopping expedition to the village when he drifted in
and slumped into a chair. He looked terrible—much
worse than he had looked last night, haggard and
exhausted.

Kate had kept the coffee hot and now, judging his
need, she put a mug of *café au lait* in front of him. He
gulped it down and lifted a bleary eye. 'Where is he?
Where's the nearly fiancé?' he growled.

Kate arranged her purse and the milk can in her basket
neatly before she replied. 'He's gone,' she said.

He gave her a weary look. 'What do you mean—
"gone"?'

'Gone—left—returned to London. Any more questions?' She turned to the door.

He ran a hand through his tangled black hair. 'Kate,
be merciful, don't keep me in suspense. Do you mean
it's over?'

'Yes,' she said brightly. 'It's over, done with. We found
we were—what's the word?—incompatible.'

A delighted grin stretched Will's mobile mouth. He
was on his feet, the weariness gone. He took the basket
from her and laid it on the table. Then he put both arms
round her. 'Kate—my beautiful, clever Kate, that's the
wisest thing you've ever done in your life.
Congratulations.' He kissed her soundly and rubbed his
bristly chin against her cheek.

'Ouch! Stop!' She pulled away, laughing, filled with
a sudden euphoria. Things were right between them
again.

He went back to the table and finished his coffee,
standing up. 'I shall go and make myself presentable,
and then a new chapter will begin, won't it? *Won't it?*'

'Perhaps,' said Kate cautiously, but her eyes were
dancing. 'But hadn't you better work on the chapters of
your book, rather than any other chapter?'

'Finished!' he said in triumph. 'Finished around five
o'clock this morning. I just went on and on until I came

to the end. I was so damned miserable last night that there didn't seem anything else to do. You'd been out all day with that fellow, and then when I saw him going upstairs and casting a languishing look at you, waiting for you to follow, I could have . . . well, never mind now. Just say I felt murderous.'

'It wasn't a languishing look,' Kate said. 'Reproachful, rather. I think he thought I'd let him down.'

'And had you?'

'Certainly not. I'd been out with him a few times, but that was all.'

He digested that slowly. 'So—the night before, you didn't—you weren't . . . ?' He came close, towering over her.

She laughed up at him. 'You're jealous.'

'As hell,' he admitted.

She pushed him towards the door. 'Go and get shaved,' she said. 'You alarm me when you look so fierce.'

He growled horribly, kissed her again. Then he held her away and gazed into her eyes. 'Oh, Kate, darling, you've no idea how relieved I am. One big hurdle is removed. We can start a new chapter. Don't go away; I won't be long.'

When he had gone Kate sat down and drew in a long breath. A new chapter? Yes, it did seem like that. She and Will were going to be together for she didn't know how long, but at the moment it didn't seem to matter. Nothing mattered in this new, exciting world that she was entering except that they wanted each other. She hummed cheerfully as she went upstairs and stripped the bed that Edward had slept in last night, and looked round the room. He had left it fastidiously tidy.

Downstairs again she made more coffee and set breakfast for Will. He looked so thin, poor darling; she was sure he didn't look after himself properly. She must find out whether he had a housekeeper or . . . Her thoughts suddenly took a new and ominous turn. What had he meant when he had said that one hurdle had been removed? How many others were there—and did they include another woman?

She pushed the thought away firmly. He'd tell her in his own good time, and, whatever it was, it mustn't be allowed to spoil things for them.

He looked a different man when he came back. He had showered and shaved. Beads of water glistened on his dark hair. He came straight to her and took her in his arms. 'Now,' he said, 'I can kiss you properly,' and he rubbed his smooth chin against her face.

It was heaven to be in his arms, bliss to feel his kisses on her mouth. She kissed him back hungrily, and ripples of excitement thrilled through her. She was lost in a new world of pure sensation.

She felt him begin to tremble. 'Darling,' he muttered against her lips, 'could you—could we . . . ?' He let her go, shaking his head. 'No, I mustn't ask you. It's too soon.'

Kate's legs sagged and she half fell into the nearest chair. Will had walked over to the window and from what seemed a long way away she heard him swear explosively. At the same moment there was the sound of a car pulling up outside.

'If that's that blasted sausage fellow turned up at last,' Will muttered, 'I'm going to . . .'

Kate took a deep, steadying breath and joined Will at the window in time to see a plump, dapper little man getting out of the car, waving to the driver, and approaching the front door. 'I believe it is,' she said, giggling feebly. 'He looks a bit like a sausage, doesn't he? But we mustn't make fun of him.'

She ran to the front door and Will followed.

'Pierre Boudin,' the little man announced. '*Bonjour, mademoiselle.* I am arrived at last, and at your service. I am sorry to be so late. I am instructed to speak your language, but I fear my English is not very good.'

'Don't worry,' Kate said, smiling at the little man, whom she liked already. 'This gentleman, Monsieur Raven, is a guest here, and he will explain everything to you.'

She looked pleadingly up at Will. 'Once again I'm in your hands.'

He grinned. 'I wish you were,' he said under his breath and then stepped forward and began to talk to the Frenchman.

After preliminaries, they all went inside and Will took Pierre into the office.

'I'll get your room ready for you,' Kate said, adding to Will in an undertone, 'I'd better put Monsieur Boudin in the manager's room—the one you've been using. Do you think you'll be able to manage the stairs now?'

'Certainly.' He winked at her. 'May I have a room very close to yours?'

Kate blushed deeply and hoped the new manager wouldn't notice the undercurrent that was flowing between Will and herself.

Hastily she dismantled the small bedroom at the end of the corridor and carried Will's things upstairs. After a moment's hesitation she decided to put him in the room next to hers. Why not? she asked herself, her heart fluttering. What was going to happen would happen anyway; she couldn't stop it now.

Kate's feet seemed to dance above the ground as she set off for the village a short time later. At last everything seemed to be coming right. Will had phoned for news of the injured boy, whose name was Maurice, and been told that he was out of danger and his mother was with him. That was a great relief.

Another weight off her mind was that she had finally settled the problem of Edward without, she felt sure, hurting him very much.

And best of all she was in love and the man she loved loved her—she was almost sure he did. He had said so, and maybe she should believe him. He had also said that he intended to marry her, and that was enough for the moment.

It was a heavenly morning. The sun warmed her shining red mane of hair; the breeze that kissed her cheeks bore the scent of spring and growing things. The sky was bluer than blue, the fields greener then green, and even the black and white cows seemed to be joining in the spring promise as they munched away contentedly. She smiled happily at everyone she met in the village, whether she knew them or not, as she went from place to place, filling up her basket. Even the rather grumpy lady at the farm dairy had a pleasant '*Bonjour, mademoiselle*,' as she filled the can with creamy milk. How lovely, Kate thought, to get your milk from a real dairy in a can instead of one of those cardboard packets that slopped out when you tried to open them. It was worth the trouble of scalding the can each time you used it.

Back at the hotel Kate started to prepare lunch for the three of them. Will came in as she was spreading out a clean yellow cloth. 'Everything's sorted out,' he said and, with a glance over his shoulder, 'Our little sausage is a treasure. He's quite up to taking things over from now on—which sets us free to amuse ourselves. Isn't that a happy thought, sweetheart?' He put an arm possessively round her shoulder.

Green eyes danced up into his as Kate pulled away. 'Don't—what will he think? You're supposed to be a guest and I'm supposed to be the acting proprietor, isn't that so?'

'Well, not exactly,' Will said. 'I think our sausage has got the hang of the position—between us, I mean.'

'Oh, he has, has he? And from now on we forget the "sausage" and call him Pierre,' she added severely.

'Whatever you say, *mademoiselle*. And I love your eyes when they shine like that.' Will dropped a quick kiss on each eye in turn. 'Is his room ready? I'll take him and his bag along.'

'All ready. And perhaps you'd like to go up and find your own new room. It's the second one along at the top of the stairs. I'll get on with the lunch.'

She wasn't going to go up with him because she knew what would happen if she did. As usual, Will was following her thought process with no effort and, with a wry glance at the heightened colour in her cheeks, he grinned knowingly at her and went off to find Pierre.

Kate smiled in a bright, hostessy fashion at the two men as they came in for lunch. After Pierre had made several awkward attempts at complimenting her in English on the colourful salads and assortment of cheeses she had set out, she said, 'Please, both of you, do speak in French, and if you speak slowly I'll try to follow what you say. It'll be good practice for me.'

She looked across the table at Will. 'I mean to learn to speak French, you know.'

The black eyes glittered into hers. 'That's one of the things I'll be delighted to teach you. Just one of them.'

Really, the man was incorrigible, Kate thought, trying to pretend she hadn't heard that remark as she plied Pierre with the cheeseboard. But her heart was dancing inside her.

When lunch was over, Will said, 'Pierre has offered to look after things here for the afternoon, Kate, so that we can have a little trip together. I want particularly to go down to the beaches. It's a kind of sentimental journey and I should like it very much if you'd come with me. That OK with you, Pierre?'

'*Mais certainement, monsieur*. I seet in the office and take calls.' With a courteous bow he departed.

'You will come, won't you, darling?' Will said, and there was a strange urgency in his voice. 'Pierre really is capable of dealing with things. He knows about the accident and the insurance and everything.'

'Yes, of course, I'd love to come,' Kate said. 'I'll go up and get ready. I'll be with you in ten minutes.'

Up in her room Kate pulled off her jeans and jumper, opened the wardrobe, and surveyed the clothes she had brought with her. She selected a leisure suit in a deep cream colour. It was made of a fleecy, brushed material and would be warm enough to wear on the beach. Sensible walking shoes and a a cheeky little corduroy beret rakishly pulled over her luxurious red hair completed her outfit. She twirled before the mirror. Not bad, she thought, not bad at all. She wanted to look nice for Will, to look—lovable. She hoped he'd approve.

As she walked down the stairs she saw him waiting for her at the bottom and his eyes told her all she wanted to know.

'You look stunning,' he said. 'Like a very beautiful, huggable little teddy bear.' He proceeded to demonstrate until Kate, out of breath, pleaded for mercy.

'I wish I'd brought some decent clobber with me,' Will said as they walked to the garage. 'I didn't expect to be escorting a beautiful lady.'

'Don't worry.' She smiled up at him. 'The magpie look is all the rage this season.' He was wearing his black trousers and a thick-knit white sweater.

He saluted jauntily. 'Thanks, *mademoiselle*. Come on, then, let's be off. May we take Becky's car again, do you think? I like driving you, and my insurance covers any car I drive, if you're wondering about that.'

'I'm sure Becky won't mind,' Kate said, 'and your long legs will fit better into her car than into my Metro.'

Will seemed to know the road to the coast. 'You've been here before?' Kate asked him. She wondered what he had meant by a 'sentimental journey' and hoped he would tell her. They must start to get to know each other now; she wanted to know every little things about him—

everything he would tell her. No doubt he wouldn't tell her about the 'last hurdle'. She was sure it was another woman. She would try not to mind—anyway, she was in the past now, whoever she was.

'We're making for Arromanches,' he told her. 'I've been here many times. I always visit the beaches when I'm in these parts. Arromanches is where the British troops landed in 1944. My father was among them; he was only seventeen.'

Will was silent after this, his face set in serious lines, and Kate was content to snuggle down beside him and watch the way his long, slim fingers handled the wheel. He drove the way he did everything else—in a confident, relaxed way, content to amble along when the road was clear and speed up when he spied a car in front. Then he gave the powerful Renault her head and swished past the other car, making Kate chuckle as she recognised the usual male satisfaction of superior power. There was little traffic on the road, and anyway, she felt quite safe with him. She would always feel safe with him, she thought happily.

They made good time and surprisingly soon Kate thought she could smell the sea. Sure enough, five minutes later they were on the outskirts of Arromanches, which was larger than she had expected.

'It's grown a lot since it made history in 1944,' Will said. 'They do a big thing in tourism now. There's a museum where they've got everything—miniatures of the huge artificial ports that were built for the landings, films and talking documents in several languages, blown-up photographs of the weapons. The whole place has been turned into a legend. But I think we'll skip all that. I much prefer to walk along the beach and use my imagination as to how it was.'

Kate nodded. She could understand that.

Even so early in the season there was quite a crowd of sightseers milling around the museum. Will parked the car and they wandered away across the sand and down to the sea.

'This is a favourite holiday resort,' Will said, adding with a wry grin, 'it's chock-a-block in August. It's nice to have it almost to ourselves today.'

The sea was smooth and their feet sank into the damp sand as they walked along the edge of the tide. Up to the left the sand-hills sprouted coarse grasses, and here and there was a fragment of a concrete gun-emplacement, weathered and almost worn away by age and winter tides. It was very still. There was only the forlorn cry of sea-birds and the soft splash of tiny waves breaking at their feet.

Will said, 'Quiet, isn't it? But I never come down here without an almost physical realisation of how it must have been on that day.'

Kate said, 'Your father—did he talk to you about the landings when you were a little boy?'

Will sighed and shook his head. 'Unfortunately, no. I hardly knew him—he died when I was only small. My mother told me he'd been very badly wounded at the end of the fighting and she thought he never really got over it.

'But I can imagine, in a way, how it must have been—all those men in their battle-gear pouring down the ramp from the troop-carrier, splashing through the water, stumbling up the sand into the point-blank fire of the enemy defences. I can hear it—smell it—the chaos, the yells, the ceaseless rattle and roar of the guns, the drone of planes overhead. God, it must have been ghastly. It makes one feel guilty that our generation missed it all.'

As he spoke he had quickened his step until Kate almost had to run to keep up with him.

She said, 'But your father came through it—you said that it wasn't until later that he was wounded.'

He paused and looked down at her apologetically. 'Sorry, I get rather carried away on these occasions. Perhaps I shouldn't have asked you to come.'

Kate said gently, 'I wanted to come. I want to know about your life—your family.'

They walked on, a little slower now.

Will linked his arm with hers. 'It's quite a romantic story. I don't know exactly where it all happened, but somehow my father got left behind when the advance pressed on. He wandered off in the wrong direction and was found by a Frenchman, who took him home to his family. They cared for him until he recovered and went off to follow his regiment. Eventually he was invalided out of the army and sent home to England. Twelve years later he went back to visit the landing beaches, and searched for the family who had befriended him, hardly expecting to find them. The father had died, but the wife was still there when he found the cottage, and her daughter was caring for her. The daughter had been a little girl of ten when my father stayed with them, but now she had grown into a beautiful young woman.' Will smiled tenderly. 'Perhaps you can guess what happened. My father fell in love with her and eventually, after her mother died, he married her and took her back to England. I was born in 1961. I don't remember my father all that well—I don't think he recovered completely from his war injuries. So you see why I like to visit the landing beaches. In an odd sort of way I feel closer to him there than going to put flowers on his grave in London.'

The weather was changing. There was a chill in the air and the sunlight seemed hazier, but still they walked on. Kate said, 'So your mother brought you up alone?'

'Yes, bless her. She was marvellous and I loved her dearly. After my father died she moved back to live in France but she wanted me to be half-English and I went to my father's old school in Canterbury, and later on to his old college in Oxford. But I always went back to

Paris for my holidays. So you see why I'm a half-and-half.'

'And your mother never married again?'

He walked along in silence for such a long time that she thought he wasn't going to reply. Then he said, 'She did—two years before she died. I was away in Oxford and I didn't know at the time, but she had fallen in love with a man and he with her. It was the old, old story— he wasn't free to marry. But after a time it became clear that she was suffering from a terminal illness. Then he did obtain his freedom and they married. By this time I had finished at Oxford and was able to come home. It was rather wonderful to see their happiness, but it was all too short. Two years after the wedding my mother became much worse and then——' he paused '—well, it was the beginning of the end. My stepfather was a tower of strength to both of us. I admire him immensely. I still see a good deal of him—we share an apartment in Paris and both use it when we are in France. And I have a smallish flat in Chelsea.'

He squeezed the arm within his. 'That's my life up to date. Not very thrilling, I'm afraid.'

This was the opportunity she had been waiting for. 'Not all your life, surely?' She gave him a sideways look. 'Never been married or anything?'

'Definitely no marriage. One or two ''anythings'', ended now with no hard feelings on either side.'

Ended now? So the other hurdle wasn't a woman. She wondered how she could ask him what the hurdle was, but before she could think of the words he said, 'Now you know all about me; tell me your life story.'

'Not much to tell,' Kate said. 'I, too, was brought up by my mother—my father just walked out on us both when I was fifteen.' Her voice hardened. 'But I don't want to remember that time, or talk about it. My mother, too, was pretty marvellous to me. We had no money and she worked very hard to keep us afloat and give me what

I needed. She wasn't qualified for anything and she got work in an old people's home. I wanted to skip university and get a job, but she wouldn't hear of it. She just went on working and working, longer and longer hours. Even after I could earn enough to support us both, she didn't give it up—she said she had no social life and wouldn't know what to do with herself if she didn't work. But it was too much for her in the end. Her health began to suffer and just before Christmas she got a bad attack of bronchitis and——' Kate's voice trembled '—her heart didn't stand the strain. She died a month ago.'

'Thank you for telling me,' Will said quietly. 'In an odd sort of way our lives have run parallel. Kate, I think I must—— '

'Ouch!' She stumbled and gave a little scream as her shoes were covered in icy water. 'That was idiotic.' She scurried further up the beach and shook her feet.

'It's my fault—I didn't notice that the tide was coming in,' Will said. 'Come along, let's get back before you catch a roaring cold. Look, take your shoes off and I'll carry you.'

'All that way back? Of course you won't. I'll run back to the car and keep warm. Race you!' She ran off along the sand.

Kate had long ago won the hundred-yard race at school, and now, even with water-soaked shoes, she covered the sand with headlong speed.

Then suddenly she stopped dead. She had run straight into a bank of mist which must have been coming down without her noticing. It was all round her, like a grey blanket, obscuring the sun, blotting out the sea and the sand-hills—and Will. Where was Will? Oh, heavens, how could she have forgotten? Of course Will couldn't keep up with her. He had only just reached the stage of being able to walk without a stick.

Kate stared round helplessly—and saw nothing but heavy, still, grey mist. 'Will,' she called. 'Where are you?'

Her voice seemed to echo back to her. She shivered violently. It was silly, of course. She couldn't lose him; he must be somewhere near. But she was conscious of a horrid emptiness, of an icy fear gripping her inside.

Which way to turn? 'Will,' she yelled again. 'Will—don't leave me. I'm here.'

It was like an answer to prayer when he was suddenly there, only a few paces away, coming towards her, another human being in this terrifying grey emptiness.

'Silly girl,' he panted as he reached her side. 'Why won't you let me look after you? Didn't you see the mist coming down?'

She shook her head, biting her lip, tears welling up behind her eyes. 'It was silly—I thought I was alone—lost. Just for a moment I was scared.' She laughed unsteadily. ' "Little girl lost"—very pathetic!'

She tried to turn it into a joke, but he said quite seriously, 'I'll never lose you, Kate. I'll always be there when you call.'

Then his arms were round her and he was holding her close, kissing her, their faces wet with mist.

He didn't seem to be letting her go and her pulses began to beat heavily.

'Oh, Kate—my lovely Kate,' he breathed huskily in her ear. 'What you do to me!'

She threw her arms round his neck and kissed him back and pressed closer to the hardness of his body. He pushed her a little way away and she felt his fingers fumbling with the zip of her suit, his breath coming in little gasps. Then he had it open and his hand closed over her swelling breast and she uttered a little cry of pleasure that was almost pain. He was muttering her name under his breath as he began to move against her and waves of heat were spreading inside her until she hardly knew where she was and what was happening. She was only aware of a feeling of complete rightness, of a joining together that was natural and yet very strange—the two

of them clinging to each other in this thick, enclosing
bank of mist that blotted out everything else in the world.

Then, with a shock of disbelief, she realised that Will
wasn't holding her any longer, and heard him make a
funny, choky noise that was almost like suppressed
laughter, and she opened her eyes wide. The bank of
mist had rolled away and the beach was there again, as
clear as it had been before. In the near distance a family
party was approaching, the children shouting and
skipping on ahead. As Kate hurriedly struggled to pull
up her zip, she saw two large seagulls perched on a pro-
truding ledge of stone, only a few yards from where she
and Will were standing, eyeing them both with great
interest.

Kate began to laugh, too, and then they were laughing
together quite immoderately.

At last Will wiped his eyes and said, 'That was what
is known in the trade as an anticlimax—something
writers are taught to avoid. I think it's a sign that we
had better get back to the hotel and get you dry before
I make any more grave errors.'

She felt a little chilled by the words, even though he
was speaking lightly. 'Was it a grave error?' she said.

'Could be, could be,' he replied in quite a matter-of-
fact voice. 'We'll have to wait and see.' He tucked her
arm through his. 'Come along, back to the car, and get
those wet shoes off.'

She let him hurry her back to the car, telling herself
that he was anxious for her well-being, afraid that she
would catch cold. But she couldn't help wondering how
he could switch over so quickly from those minutes of
rising passion to a purely practical matter.

She was positive that he wanted her, just as she wanted
him. But he was putting up some barrier, real or imaginary, between them.

As she climbed into the car beside him she promised herself that, whatever it was, she was going to break it down.

CHAPTER NINE

ONCE they were in the car Will became very kind and very brisk. 'Off with those wet shoes now,' he said. 'Come on, let me help.' He leaned over and pulled off her sodden shoes, one by one, and dropped them on the back seat. 'Stretch out your legs, and when we get going I'll turn the heater on to "low" position. That should dry you off nicely.'

It did. As the car bowled along Kate lay back luxuriously and let the heat drift upwards, enveloping her in a warm glow.

Will didn't seem disposed to talk. On the way to the coast he had driven at a leisurely pace, but now he was in a different mood. He let the speedy car have her head and surprisingly soon they were pulling up in front of the hotel.

Will came round and opened the passenger door. 'I'll carry you in,' he said. 'You'll spike your feet on the gravel, with no shoes on.'

She didn't demur. She let him hoist her up into his arms and as they crossed the forecourt she reached up and rubbed her cheek against his.

He held her closer and dropped a kiss on her hair. It's going to be all right, Kate thought happily. Tonight we'll make love and then the other hurdle will be crossed, whatever it is.

Pierre Boudin must have heard the car draw up, for as they reached the front door he flung it open. Then he saw Kate being carried in and waved his hands in alarm. '*Mon Dieu—encore un accident? Ce n'est pas possible!*'

Will assured him that all was well, setting Kate down at the foot of the stairs. 'You'd better go up and have a good long, hot soak,' he said, touching the sleeve of her leisure suit. 'You're pretty damp.'

'You're pretty damp, too,' Kate said. 'Shouldn't you——?'

'Oh, I'm OK,' he put in quickly. 'This gear is guaranteed to withstand any amounts of sea-mist.' He shook himself like a terrier, and beads of water sprayed out of the thick-knit sweater. 'Anyway, I've got some work to do on the word processor—revising my script—if that's OK with you, Pierre?'

The two men went into the office, chatting, and Kate climbed slowly upstairs. She had had an idea that he might come up with her and then...but he obviously didn't intend to, and that was that. She would have to wait.

She lay in the hot water and tried to imagine what the final hurdle could be. A dark thought occurred to her. Not a health hazard, surely? No, she couldn't believe that. Will was too honourable to let things go this far if that had been the case. The only other thing she could think of was that he had decided he had been too hasty in talking about marriage—that he was regretting he had ever mentioned the word. Well, that was all right—she hadn't really made up her mind that she wanted to get married yet, had she?

Liar, of course you have. You want to marry Will Raven and nobody else in the world.

Admitting that seemed to clear her mind. If you wanted something as vitally important as marriage to a special man you went all out to get it. But as she wrapped herself in a huge warm towel she had to admit to herself that she wasn't the sort of girl who would hold out for marriage. If Will had set his face against a total commitment, she would have to settle for less. Lots of girls did in this modern, equal society.

In her bedroom she dried her hair and brushed it into
a shining fall that reached nearly to her shoulders. She
had thought about putting it up, but that would be too
much of a reminder of that awful first encounter with
Will when he had taken her for a servant girl on the
make. Not the best dress, either. She settled for an oyster-
coloured jersey skirt and top which hugged her figure
nicely without being in the least seductive—or so she
thought. But what she did do before she went downstairs was to look out the prettiest, flimsiest nightie she
had brought with her, a peach-coloured lacy chiffon, and
lay it out on the bed, feeling a warm, excited glow steal
over her as she did so. She was sure what the night would
bring, and she couldn't wait.

When she arrived downstairs, Will was nowhere to be
seen, but Pierre was in the kitchen, wrapped in a large
white apron. He really did remind her of one of those
pale-skinned sausages she had had at the hotel on previous visits.

He greeted her amiably. 'I 'ave found thees.' He
tweaked the apron. 'Monsieur Weel is busy, but I make
you a nice dinner, wiz ze Vallée d'Auge sauce, wiz butter,
cream, apples and Calvados,' he announced proudly.

'Sounds delicious,' Kate told him. 'It is very kind of
you, Monsieur Boudin.'

'Eet is my pleasure,' he told her earnestly, 'and will
you plees call me Pierre?' He turned back to the pot on
the cooker.

Kate hung around for a few minutes, but as Pierre
neither needed nor welcomed any assistance she left him
to it.

The door of the office was ajar and she glanced in.
Will was huddled over the computer. She stood watching
him, loving the way his dark hair grew down into his
neck. It gave her a small thrill to remember the way her
fingers had tangled into his hair down on the beach.
And tonight again...

He was concentrating hard and she knew she mustn't disturb him. She wondered if he would let her read the manuscript of his new book—that would be wonderful.

It would be fun, she thought, to be married to—or, anyway, living with—a real writer. She would enjoy sharing the ups and downs of a writer's life, she was sure she would. She wondered if he did his writing in London. If so, she would look for another job. But if he lived mostly in Paris, that might be more difficult. Perhaps he'd let her help him with the typing of his manuscript, and at the same time she would begin to learn French. She began to plan happily and went into the lounge, switched on the TV, and tried to make out the news bulletin. Life was going to be so full of new, wonderful things. She couldn't wait for it to begin.

The three of them had dinner together. Pierre had set a table in the dining-room. The cutlery was gleaming and he had found clean napkins. In the middle of the table was the little vase of flowers she had picked for Edward. How glad she was that she wasn't dining with Edward tonight!

The dinner was an almost festive occasion. Pierre had found some shellfish in the freezer and this, annointed with his Normandy-style sauce, was really delicious. The little man flushed with pleasure when Will and Kate were enthusiastic in praise of his cooking. Will seemed in high spirits. He had, he told Kate, finally completed the revision of his book, and he asked Kate if she thought Becky would mind if he borrowed the floppy disk he'd been using to send it to his usual secretarial bureau for its final printing.

Kate laughed and said that she would sure Becky would agree to anything now it had finally been decided that she was going to leave hospital in two days.

'It was nice of her doctor friend to phone and let us know,' she said, 'and to invite me to visit Becky at his home in Caen. I'll certainly take him up on that . . . I'm dying to see Becky again.'

'Let's drive into Caen together when Becky is there,' Will suggested. 'When you've finished your visit we could go on to Giverny. I'm determined to show you the water-gardens.'

'Oh, that would be fine.' Kate's eyes met Will's in a long, understanding look that sent little shivers up and down her spine. So many lovely things in store for them!

After dinner she insisted on washing up and tidying the kitchen and she shooed the two men into the lounge with their coffee and Calvados. 'You've both been in-valids recently,' she laughed. 'Now you must let me do my whack.'

She spun out the washing-up, wanting to fill in the time until she could reasonably go up to bed.

When she got back to the lounge she found the two men deep in conversation. Will smiled at her and patted the place next to him on the sofa. 'Pierre is telling me all about the life of a hotel manager,' he told her. 'It's quite fascinating and it's given me an idea for my next book.' He grinned and added, 'I believe we writers were all squirrels in an earlier existence. Every little nut of experience is carefully hoarded for later digging up and using when it will come in handy.' He turned to Pierre and translated and Pierre roared with laughter.

Kate didn't really want to hear about squirrels or a former existence—she was much too concerned about what was going to happen next in this one. Earlier she had been sure that tonight she and Will would share the same bed, but at the moment he seemed in no hurry to arrange it. Pierre went on talking in French and Will went on listening, apparently with every sign of enjoyment.

Will had put his arm around Kate while they talked, and she began to get more and more edgy. She could feel the warmth of his body through his shirt and the

closeness of him was having a terrible effect on her.
Although he went on listening with apparent interest to
Pierre, she knew beyond a doubt that he was feeling the
same way. His hand gripped her waist tighter and tighter,
the fingers spreading out and closing again, and she felt
a tiny shiver pass through him now and again. When
she couldn't bear it any longer she stood up, yawning
delicately. 'Well, I think I'm for bed, so I'll say goodnight to the two of you.'

Pierre wished her a beaming, *'Bonne nuit,
mademoiselle. Dormez bien.'* She escaped quickly upstairs before Will had a chance to say anything at all.

In her bedroom Kate sat down on the edge of the bed.
She was cold as ice and her limbs were trembling un-
controllably. This was ridiculous, she told herself.
Modern young women didn't behave like shy Victorian
brides facing the unknown terrors of wedding-night
nerves. Did they?

It wasn't even as if she were a virgin. Memory slipped
back to a night at a college dance when she had drunk
too much wine and had felt excited and rather flattered
to find herself in bed with the good-looking boy who
was the current heart-throb, as it was called then, of her
class.

All the other girls were sleeping with their boyfriends,
she knew that, and she had felt rather left out of their
mutual confidences. Now, as she rather enjoyed the
heart-throb's preliminary kisses, she had thought hazily,
Why not?

The heart-throb had turned out to be both clumsy and
selfish and she hadn't enjoyed what followed. Certainly
she'd never been tempted to repeat the experience.

After she left college and got her first job there had
been no time for a social life and boyfriends. Every hour
of her day had been filled.

The memory of those difficult days passed before her
eyes as if they were happening now: herself hurrying

home after work to find Mother, pale and exhausted,
struggling to cook a meal for them both before she went
back to do an extra evening shift at the old people's
home. After a time their life had settled down into a
dreary pattern and Kate had given up all idea of having
a life of her own. She was almost painfully aware of
what her mother had sacrificed to put her through
college, to buy the clothes she needed in order to 'hold
up her head' among her contemporaries, to keep the flat
'nice' so that Kate could invite her friends home. When
Mother's health had begun to show signs of weakening,
although her obsessive need to go on working had not,
Kate had taken over more and more of the work that
had to be done.

Pictures came into her mind as she sat on the bed:
herself pushing her trolley round the supermarket in the
evenings; lugging their washing to the launderette because there was nowhere in the flat to hang it to dry;
ironing everything to meet Mother's high standards;
sharing the cleaning, the washing-up, sharing the
hundred and one small jobs that Mother found essential
round the flat. And that awful last phase after Mother's
health had finally broken down and Kate had had to
give up her job...

Suddenly she shivered violently and pushed the memories away. Her life was her own now and she knew what
she wanted to do with it.

She wanted Will—with or without marriage—and she
was sure he meant to come to her, to finish what they
had started on the beach, enclosed in their curtain of
mist.

She got up and washed her face, cleaned her teeth,
and brushed her hair. Then she undressed, slipped the
filmy nightie over her head, and lay down in the big,
soft bed, pulling the duvet up to her chin.

Time crawled by. She would know when Will came
up because the stairs creaked. The bedside light was on,

and she had left the door open a crack so that he would know she was awake.

It seemed that hours passed, but at last she started up in bed as she heard the floorboards on the stairs creak. She held her breath, her heart thumping painfully.

Now he had reached the top of the stairs; he was turning the corner. She could sense his presence as he came nearer and nearer. He had reached her door now.

Then—he had walked straight past it, not pausing for a second. She heard the door of his own room close behind him.

She couldn't believe it. She'd been so certain that he would come to her. Everything that had happened today had made her more certain. Then why? It must be this 'last hurdle' that was holding him back, and she had got to find out what it was. Now, this moment.

She went cold inside and she started to shake again as she knew what she must do, but nothing was going to stop her now.

Before she had time to think she flung herself out of bed, threw a wrap over her nightdress, and was across the room and outside Will's door in a matter of seconds.

Here she paused to draw a quick breath and then knocked resolutely. There was no response. She waited and knocked again—he was probably in the shower-room. She opened the door and walked in. At the same moment Will emerged from the shower-room. He was naked except for a green towel knotted round his waist, and in the dim light from the bedside lamp he looked magnificent—larger than life. Kate felt a weakness behind her ribs at the sight of his gleaming body, fresh from the shower, smooth and biscuit-coloured, with a streak of black hair dividing his chest down to his navel.

She made a tremendous effort to remember what she'd come for. She cleared her throat nervously. 'Will—I think we ought to talk.'

'Do you?' he said softly, walking towards her. The eyes that looked into hers were black pools, the voice a low, caressing, heart-stopping sound. 'Do you indeed? What a waste of time talking would be, don't you agree?'

He was very close now, but he didn't touch her. He said wryly, 'It's just taken an enormous effort to stop myself from coming into your room and pouncing on you. I've even taken a cold shower——' he shivered histrionically '—but it hasn't done much good. And now, here you are—where you belong.' His arms went round her, holding her loosely.

His voice dropped to a velvety caress. 'Oh, my darling, adorable, beautiful Kate, there's only one thing we can do now, and that isn't talk. Yes?'

She had forgotten all about hurdles. 'Yes,' she whispered. 'Oh, Will, yes.'

His hands were on her shoulders. 'I don't think we need this,' he said, and she could hear the smile in his voice as the thin wrap slid to the floor. 'Or this.' He pulled up the nightdress a little way, then paused with an indrawn breath, before the nightdress finally joined the wrap on the floor. The towel round his waist had already been discarded and he took her fully into his arms, drawing her against him with murmured words of tenderness and desire that sounded beautiful in her ears.

Carefully he lifted her and laid her on the wide bed, pushing aside the coverlet. Then he was beside her, lifting himself on one elbow, gazing down into her eyes.

He said solemnly, 'I'd never do anything to harm you, my darling. You believe that?'

She nodded speechlessly.

'In the very deepest part of me I love you, Kate. And you?'

She nodded again.

'Say it,' he insisted.

'I love you, Will. I do love you very much.'

'And you'll marry me?'

She shouldn't have doubted, she thought hazily. 'Yes,' she said.

She felt him relax beside her. 'Then what are we waiting for?' he said with a broken laugh and his mouth was on hers at last.

He must have realised that she wasn't really experienced, she thought, for he roused her slowly and tenderly, his mouth trailing over her body, releasing exquisite stabs of pleasure that was almost pain, so that she let out little startled gasps as her body arched itself against him.

He wasn't a silent lover; he spoke endearments against her lips, against the peaks of her breasts, telling her how beautiful and desirable she was to him, and she sank deeper and deeper into a warm sea of ecstasy that she had only guessed at before.

As his kisses became more urgent she moved against him, following her sure impulses, letting her own hands touch him, explore him, making him cry out sharply.

'Please—please,' she heard herself beg as her need spilled out of her and then at last she felt his weight on her and she gave a groan of wonder as they were linked together at last.

Then it was an all too short time of rising passion, of gasps and cries, of plunging and thrusting and a kind of wild tumult that engulfed them both until it rose to a final, long-drawn-out explosion and they collapsed in each other's arms, panting for breath.

'Wonderful—marvellous…' Will muttered. 'The very best.'

And for answer Kate sagged against him and let her hand lie across his flat stomach, warm and damp and silky, as was her own skin. 'I—never—knew…' Her voice trailed off and she slept.

She wakened to see the sunlight creeping in round the edges of the pink damask curtains. With a drowsy sigh of pure happiness she stretched out an arm to Will, but her hand encountered nothing but the crumpled bed-clothes, and they weren't even warm. He had gone.

For a ghastly moment fear gripped her stomach. She pulled herself up in the bed, telling herself that it was all right; he had got up early, that was all it was. But she had to see him, to hear his voice, to reassure herself that last night hadn't been a dream.

In her own room next door she showered quickly, pulled on jeans and sweater, tugged a brush through her hair, and ran downstairs.

She didn't meet Pierre, but Will was in the kitchen, waiting for the kettle to boil. His face lit up at the sight of her and he put his arms tightly round her and kissed her.

'Good morning, darling.' His smile reassured her that everything was all right, that last night really had happened.

The kettle boiled and he made tea. 'I was going to surprise you,' he said. 'I wakened early and watched you sleeping and I soon got ideas. But I couldn't bring myself to waken you up—you looked so peaceful—so I did the noble thing and came down to make you tea instead.'

She chuckled and looked up at him through her lashes. 'There's such a thing as being too noble,' she said demurely and he had to kiss her again after that.

His mouth trailed down to her neck and rested there. 'Shall we forget about the tea?' he whispered.

Kate's green eyes sparkled as she said sedately, 'Certainly not, I'm thirsty—and hungry.'

'Oh, well——' Will pulled a face at her '—I'm hungry too. Being in love doesn't take one's appetite away as we're led to believe. I shall scramble eggs for us.'

Breakfast was a hilarious meal with a great deal of good-natured teasing. Kate thought she'd never been so happy in all her life.

They washed the dishes together, then Kate looked out of the window and stretched her arms wide. 'What a glorious morning. Let's go for a walk. I'll take you up the lane—the little lane that the hotel took its name from—you know, Farm of the Green Lane. I daren't pronounce it in French or you'd make fun of my accent.'

Will insisted on her saying '*Ferme du Chemin Vert*' over and over until he approved. Then he had to kiss her as a reward. They were like two children—or two lovers, Kate thought. Being in love took all the bad years away somehow.

The lane was narrow and rutted, with high, tangled hedges and trees that almost met overhead. Kate had always loved the lane and had a childish idea of it as a hidden secret place. She'd never found out where it led— if, indeed, it led anywhere at all.

As the strolled along, arm in arm, Kate said, 'I've often walked here with Becky. In the summer when the leaves are out the trees meet overhead and it's like walking through a cool green tunnel. Lovely!'

'Lovely!' Will echoed absently. He was silent for a time and then he said suddenly, 'Kate, was I too rough with you last night? I'm afraid I got carried away. I needed it so badly and you were so wonderfully responsive.'

She smiled softly. This morning she felt she could say anything to Will; there was no barrier between them. She said, 'I think I needed it too. I never knew that sex could be like that—it sort of takes you over.'

'It needn't always be so frantic. Sometimes it can be quiet and deeply satisfying.'

Before she had time to wonder about the other women he'd made love to he went on quickly, 'Oh, darling Kate, isn't it splendid to think we've got weeks—months— years—ahead of us? All our lives together.' He hugged her close and she rubbed her cheek against his shoulder.

'And in the end,' she said, 'it didn't matter about that last hurdle. You decided that you did want to get married after all.'

He stopped walking, turned her round, and stared into her face in puzzlement. 'What are you talking about? I've always wanted to marry you. I did right from the beginning, I think, when I got out of the taxi and you greeted me so charmingly in very bad French. You said *"que vous avez arrivé"* and it should have been *"que vous êtes arrivé"*. End of lesson.'

'I'll try to remember, sir,' she said meekly. 'But what was the hurdle? You've made me curious.'

He looked down at the ground and kicked a stone out of the day. 'I started to tell you on the beach yesterday, but you walked into the sea, and after that everything happened rather quickly. And last night—I was sure we were very soon going to make love and I didn't want it to happen before you knew. I thought it wouldn't be fair to you. Then you took things into your own hands and——' he shrugged '—I'm only a mere man.'

Kate was conscious of a chill in the breeze that blew along the lane. 'Before I knew what?'

He gave an embarrassed laugh. 'This sounds rather ridiculous, but it isn't really.' He paused again for a long time and then his mouth twisted into an odd smile. 'It seems, Kate, darling, that I'm your stepbrother. Your father married my mother two years before she died.'

'What?' The sound came from somewhere outside herself. 'It isn't true. Say it isn't true.'

She pulled away from him and stepped back and her legs felt numb and heavy. Her eyes stared.

'It's true,' Will said, 'but it needn't make any difference to us. We're not blood relations, of course, and now that we know we love each other nothing else really matters. You don't have to see your father unless—until—you really want to. But I know how much it means to Jimbo.'

'Jimbo?' Who was he talking about?

'We always called your father "Jimbo". It was my mother's pet name for him.' He stopped, his eyes tender for just a moment. 'They were very much in love.'

'Really?' She was beginning to feel very calm now that the first shock was over. Very calm and very cold.

'Look, darling,' Will pleaded, 'do you have to be like this? I know how much you mean to your father. All the years I've known him he's talked about you. He has your photograph beside his bed.'

'Very touching!' Kate sneered. She hardly knew what she was saying. Her world was crumbling into pieces around her, and Will had turned into an enemy, an enemy who had planned and schemed to make her accept something her whole being revolted against.

Will was going on talking—being reasonable. He must think he was winning her over.

'He's longing to see you again. Whatever you may think, he loves you very much.'

Kate said through stiff lips, 'So he sent you to find out what sort of a girl I've grown into, to spy on me. Have you been phoning back reports to him while I've been out shopping?'

'Don't be so idiotic.' Will was beginning to lose patience. 'Of course I haven't. He's in Japan on a business trip. And anyway, he didn't know you'd be here, that I should actually meet you. He merely suggested that I should come here to convalesce, and to make myself known to Becky, from whom I could find out how you were, and if you were at all disposed to see him. He knows quite well that your mother would have worked on you to turn you against him and blacken his name in your eyes.'

Kate flared up, the coldness suddenly turned to blazing anger. 'What a disgusting thing to say! My mother didn't have to work on me. The facts were there for me to see. The night before he left he told me he loved me. The next day he was gone and I never heard a word from him again. He left us penniless and my mother worked herself to death to support us both. What sort of love is that?' The words tumbled over one another.

Bill stared at her incredulously. 'Left you penniless? No, I can't believe that of him.'

'Well, you'd better believe it, because it's true. He's cruel and heartless and I never want to see him again.' Her throat choked up. 'Or you, either.'

'Kate—darling—you don't mean that—you can't. Not after what we've had together. Not after you said you love me.' His face had had turned ashen under his smooth, faintly tanned skin. 'But why?'

Kate pulled herself together. She had to finish this quickly. 'What we had together was merely sex,' she said almost calmly. Her lips curled in contempt. 'I suppose you thought you'd be a clever little peacemaker, and have a little bit of fun on the side, was that it?'

'No,' he shouted violently. He took a step towards her, his face working furiously, and for a moment she had a terrifying feeling that he was going to strike her. But he drew back and said more quietly, 'That's unfair and untrue, and you damn well know it, Kate. And anyway,' he added, his mouth dragging down at the corners, 'if that was what I wanted I'd have taken it days ago, and you'd have liked it. And I seem to remember that it wasn't I who made the first move last night, and that you said you loved me.'

His eyes searched her face as if to find some sign of understanding.

'Last night I didn't know you. I thought you were honest and straightforward. But it seems I was wrong. You've lied and cheated right from the first. You must have known who I was. You should have told me.'

'And then you'd have thrown me out, wouldn't you?'

She turned her head away. 'Probably,' she said distantly.

He took a step towards her. 'Kate—sweetheart—surely we can clear this up. You don't have to take it with such deadly seriousness.' He put a hand on her arm pleadingly.

'Don't touch me.' She shrank away from him, backing into an old wooden gate in the hedge. 'We can't clear it up. It's over. I don't want to see you—or my father, who you think so marvellous—ever again. You're two of a kind. You can go back and tell him that.'

She drew herself up to her full height. She couldn't last out much longer. 'And I'd be glad if you would arrange to leave as soon as possible.'

She couldn't meet his eyes, although she knew he was staring at her as the silence between them got colder and colder.

At last he said stonily, 'Very well, I'll go and pack, and arrange for transport. Please ask Pierre to prepare my bill.' He turned on his heel and limped back along the lane to the hotel, leaving Kate feeling more alone than she had ever felt in her life.

CHAPTER TEN

KATE leaned back against the broken gate, conscious of nothing but an empty, sick feeling in her stomach, a leadenness in her limbs.

The gate sagged under her weight and she slid to the ground, catching at the hedge as she fell, tearing her hands on the brambles. She kept on moaning softly, 'No—no—no—not again—it couldn't happen again.'

After a time she turned over and managed to lever herself up. She felt stiff and helpless, like an old, old woman.

She saw that on the other side of the gate a group of cows was grazing in a field, too close for comfort. She dragged the broken gate into place as best she could, wondering vaguely where to go. She couldn't go back to the hotel, where she might meet Will. There was only one way, and that was onwards along the lane.

Walking was difficult; she kept catching her toes in the ruts and once she fell forward heavily on to her knees and lay whimpering with pain and frustration. When she managed to get up she saw that her jeans were torn and her knee was bleeding, but there was nothing she could do about it so she plodded on doggedly.

She didn't recognise this part of the lane; she had never come as far as this with Becky on their evening strolls. But any lane must lead somewhere eventually. Perhaps it would come out into the village street and there might be some place where she could sit down and ask for a drink of water. Her mouth was dry and her lips felt stiff and swollen.

But the lane narrowed and narrowed until it was little more than a path. And then it was nothing at all. A high bank, covered with brambles, barred her way. She stared hopelessly at the long straggle of stems with thorns looking vicious against the bare wood.

She couldn't walk any more. She sat down on the rough grass and allowed time to pass.

In her state of shock, Kate had no idea where the hours went to, but when she finally arrived back at the hotel she sensed that it must be mid-afternoon. To her amazement, the first person she saw, standing at the front door, was Marie, large and comfortably welcome, in a blue serge skirt and white cotton blouse. She was standing on the steps, staring anxiously up and down the road. When she saw Kate her round face lit up. 'Mees Kate— 'ow glad I am to see you!' Marie spoke English adequately and very fast. 'I am ver' puzzled. I cannot find *madame* in any place and there is a strange gentleman in the office; he says he is the new manager.'

Before Kate could explain, Marie threw up her hands in horror. 'But you are ill and you are hurt! Your hands are bleeding. What has happened? Come with me and I will attend to them.'

Kate allowed herself to be led to the downstairs cloakroom next door to the office. Will wasn't here, she thought dully. He wasn't anywhere in the hotel; if he had been she would have felt his presence. Instead there was a heavy emptiness in the whole building.

Marie was a kind, motherly soul. She clucked over Kate's torn hands and grazed knee while Kate explained about Becky, adding quickly that she was making a splendid recovery and would be back at the hotel very soon.

'Monsieur Boudin is only here while my aunt is away,' she told Marie, who was obviously highly suspicious of anyone sitting in Becky's chair in the office.

'And there was another gentleman.' Marie tied a bandage firmly around Kate's knee. 'He was in a great 'urry to leave. Jacques 'as driven him to the station, and when he returns he will clean *madame's* car, which is dirty.' Marie's sharp little eyes were curious, but Kate had no intention of explaining Will, or why the car had been used. All she wanted to do was to lie on her bed and pull the bedclothes over her head.

Marie disappeared and came back with a red dressing-gown, which she had evidently fetched from Becky's quarters in the annexe.

She helped Kate into it. 'Now you go and 'ave a nice rest while I make you some good strong coffee.' She picked up the torn jeans and muddy jumper and bustled away.

On her way upstairs Kate paused outside the office door. Had Will left any message for her, or had he walked out of the hotel and out of her life, as she had told him to?

Pierre beamed at her when she went in and then exclaimed over her bandaged hands, but Kate brushed aside what she took to be his expression of concern with a shrug and a halting, '*Ce n'est rien*', which he appeared to understand.

'Monsieur Weel 'as given this to me.' He pushed a card across the desk to her. 'To post heem ze *note.*'

'Note?' Kate frowned. 'Oh, you mean his account. She shook her head and pushed the card into the pocket of the dressing-gown. 'No, no note,' she said firmly. It was going to be impossible to communicate with Pierre; she would have to get Marie to act as interpreter.

Pierre handed her an envelope. 'From Monsieur Weel—for you,' he said.

Kate took it, her heart giving a great leap, and thrust it into her pocket with the card.

Upstairs in her room it was agony to have to wait until Marie had brought coffee and fussed round with pillows and duvet. 'Now, you must have a nice sleep, and I will cook dinner for all of us,' she said happily. She was obviously glad to be back in harness after her holiday.

When the door had closed behind her, Kate took a gulp of hot, strong coffee and tore open the envelope, her hands shaking.

On a small slip of paper Will had written in the almost illegible writer's scrawl she had come to recognise after working with him in the office:

Dear Kate,
I have taken the liberty of borrowing the floppy disk I've been using. There seem to be several spares. There hasn't been time to print it all out, as I thought it best to get myself off the premises as quickly as possible. I'll have the disk copied and return it very shortly.
                                                    Yours, Will.

Kate read the dry little note through three times. Then she sat staring blindly out of the window.

Will had gone and he wouldn't come back. In spite of his light and easygoing ways there was a pride about him that made her sure he wouldn't come back to plead. Anyway, she didn't want him back, did she? How could she? There could never be anything permanent between them, not with that dark shadow hanging in the background.

It had been merely a physical attraction, she tried to convince herself. She would miss Will badly for a while, but she would get over it in time. This heavy weight in her chest would go away eventually.

She looked down at the note again, and she seemed to see Will writing it, leaning over the desk, as she had seen him so often in the last few days. She saw his slim fingers holding the pen, his dark head bent as he wrote, his face stern and angry as she had last seen it in the lane. Then she saw something else and this wasn't imagination. In the bottom left corner was scrawled 'Over'.

She turned the slip of paper over and read:

I'm sorry I was such a disappointment to you. I wish you well always.

Love, Will

Kate sat very still. The few words were an arrow aimed straight at her heart. Then she sank back against the pillows and tenderness flooded through her like a warm stream, washing away the bitterness and resentment. 'Will—oh, Will,' she whispered brokenly. And she covered her face with her hands and began to weep.

Misery had never taken her like this before. Even in the worst of the bad days ten years ago she hadn't cried very much. She had gone on with a kind of gritty determination, probably unconsciously imitating Mother's behaviour. She'd never seen Mother cry.

But now Kate sobbed and went on sobbing and out of the deluge of misery one certainty emerged. She loved Will and nothing that he had done could change that. She loved him and she'd sent him away. She'd been stubborn and unreasonable and refused to listen to explanations. She felt icy cold as she imagined him in a train to Paris, speeding further away from her with every moment that passed, returning to his work, his friends, all his interests, pushing away the memory of a stupid girl who hadn't known her own mind, a girl who harboured old grievances and grudges and allowed them to spoil her own and other people's lives.

She was seized with a terrible urgency. She couldn't let him go like this. She must do something quickly—quickly.

Choking and hiccuping, she crawled across the room, filled the washbasin, and plunged her face into it.

The shock of the icy water cleared her mind. As she dried her face she began to think and plan. She couldn't contact Will until he got back to Paris, but meanwhile she would write a letter. A letter would be more personal and intimate than a phone call. If she couldn't reach him by phone at least he would receive the letter.

She took her pad and wrote:

Dear Will
You were right and I was wrong. We should have talked things over. I'm sorry I was such a pig, and if you can forgive me please get in touch.

Love, Kate

Will's card was in her pocket. She fished it out and addressed an envelope. She had to get it into the post as soon as she could.

She did her best with make-up to disguise the ravages of the last half-hour, put on a clean linen dress, and ran down to the office for a stamp.

Pierre was not in the office, but there was a pile of letters on the desk, waiting for the morning collection. She couldn't bear to trust her letter to this anonymous collection of business letters, and there might just be a possibility of getting it away before tomorrow.

She hadn't driven the Metro since she arrived, but it started sweetly and she drove to the village. With some difficulty she managed to find out at the shop that the postman wouldn't call until morning, and with that she had to be content. Tomorrow was Wednesday. Will would get the letter by Thursday, if she couldn't manage to reach him by phone in the meantime. She'd phone him at six o'clock; he should be home by then. Only another hour to get through.

When she arrived back at the hotel she saw a large black car standing in front of the entrance door and her heart lurched with a wild hope that Will might have come back. But the man who greeted her as she walked in was Becky's Dr Louis waiting for her.

Her jaw dropped. 'Aunt Becky? She's not worse?'

'Non, non,' the doctor assured her. 'She is well. She will leave hospital tomorrow.'

'And she will be staying with your mother?'

He shook his head dolefully. '*Je suis désolé. Maman* has a virus and it would not be safe for your aunt to be with her.'

He had come to see Kate and find out how things were at the hotel and if Becky could be allowed home without putting a strain on her.

Kate assured him that Becky would be well looked after, and not allowed to tire herself. Marie, the housekeeper, had returned, and the temporary manager was coping with the office work.

'I shall look forward to seeing her tomorrow,' Kate said, 'and we will have everything prepared for her.'

Looking happier, the doctor departed. He *was* a nice man, Kate thought, and he seemed so fond of Becky. She hoped things would go right for them.

Kate went to give Marie the good news, and together they prepared Becky's room in the annexe, where she had her own suite. This part of the hotel was modern and had been built when Becky married the hotel's previous owner. Marie dusted everything, although it had all looked spotless to start with. Kate put two paperbacks she had brought from England on the bedside table, together with a tiny posy of spring flowers. First thing in the morning they would make up the bed, Marie decided, and then all the bedclothes would be aired and warm.

Back in the kitchen they found that Jacques had returned and Kate greeted him like the old friend he was. She was longing to ask him where he had left Will and if he knew what train he intended to catch, but of course she couldn't. She would just have to be patient.

They would all eat together in the kitchen, Marie said; that would be friendly, and Kate busied herself setting the table. When she couldn't find anything else to do she went up to her room and prowled about there restlessly, picking things up and putting them down until she was almost screaming with nerves. But she wouldn't allow herself to go to the phone before six o'clock.

When her little clock told her it was one minute past six she went down to the visitors' telephone in an alcove between the lounge and the dining-room. The number of Will's Paris apartment was on the card in her pocket and she got it out with shaking hands and dialled the number before she had time to make up her mind which, of all the beginnings she had rehearsed, she was going to use. She leaned weakly against the partition, listening to the phone ringing at the other end. No reply. Perhaps she'd dialled a wrong number. She tried again with the same result. Perhaps Will was in the shower. Or perhaps he hadn't got back yet. He wouldn't come home to an empty, cold flat, would he, without having a meal? Yes, that was it; he was in a restaurant somewhere, having dinner.

Three times that evening Kate dialled Will's number, only to be greeted with the same blank silence each time. She sat alone in the lounge with the TV flickering and chattering incomprehensibly. The log fire hadn't been lit today and the heating wasn't overcoming the chill of the big room.

At half-past eleven, after another fruitless call, she dragged herself up to bed. Will had met friends; he was socialising somewhere—Paris didn't close down at night, did it?—and not giving her a thought.

Drooping with tiredness, she went upstairs and got ready for bed.

She lay in bed, wondering how she was going to pass the night. In spite of her tiredness, every nerve in her body was jangling with tension.

At one o'clock she could stand it no longer. She crept out on to the landing. The house was in darkness. Jacques and Marie had their room in a converted stable in the grounds and Pierre was doubtless fast asleep in his room at the end of the office passage. Kate crept noiselessly down the stairs. The light from her bedroom streamed down as far as the lounge and in the telephone alcove there was a light switch. One last try, she thought desperately, and dialled the number again. By now she knew it off by heart.

The phone rang, followed by the usual silence. But then there was a click and a woman's voice said sharply, 'Yes, yes, who is that?' in English.

Kate went icy cold. Lisbeth—Will's slinky agent— she'd know that voice anywhere. A second later Will's voice shouted from somewhere, 'Who is it, Lisbeth? Ask them to hang on for a minute.'

Kate's palm was wet as it gripped the receiver. She heard Lisbeth say, 'There doesn't seem to be anyone there,' and then, in a soft, cooing voice, very faint as she turned from the mouthpiece, 'Hurry, Willy-boy, I'm waiting.'

Kate replaced the receiver blindly. She saw the wide bed and Lisbeth's white-gold hair spread across the pillow, her vivid blue eyes heavy with desire. She saw Will coming from the shower, a towel round his waist, just as he had done last night...

Her head was swimming and she felt horribly sick. She stumbled into a chair and leaned forward, waiting until the faint feeling went off.

Some time later—she had no idea when—she found herself up in her bedroom without any clear idea how she had got there. She lay in the bed and stared at the ceiling. Could men do that? Make love to one girl and the following night turn to another? Apparently some men could.

What an utter, utter fool she'd been! She should never have allowed herself to be seduced from her first opinion of Will Raven by smooth talk and her own deplorable eagerness to be made love to. She went hot all over as she remembered how she had gone into his room last night simply panting to be loved. Never again, she vowed.

Never, never again. She would never believe a man again. Two betrayals were enough.

She got up and swallowed a couple of aspirin, for her head felt as if it were splintering into small pieces. Then she turned out the light and lay awake, grimly waiting for the morning to come.

By the time it was light the weather had changed. Kate lay listening to the rain lashing against the window and watching the sullen black clouds rolling across the sky. Very well timed, she thought, with an irony that was new to her. All the brightness and colour had gone out of her world too.

Her limbs were stiff and aching as she got out of bed, partly the result of the fall, but mostly the tension of the night. A warm shower helped a little. She dressed in a pair of loose navy trousers, which hid the bandage on her knee. Becky mustn't start worrying about her when she got home.

Early as she was, Marie was up before her, and together they made up the bed, all ready for Becky, while Marie chattered on about her holiday in Boulogne with her daughter-in-law, but said how glad she was to be back at the Ferme in time to welcome *madame* home from hospital. Kate went out in the rain and picked a small posy of flowers to put on the table in Becky's sitting-room, and lit a fire in the small grate which provided auxiliary heating and gave the room a cheery look.

Breakfast nearly choked her, but she listened to the other three and put a rather wooden smile on her mouth while Pierre talked amiably to Marie and Jacques.

Becky arrived home at ten o'clock, driven by the doctor, who treated her like a piece of precious porcelain, wrapping her in a rug and trotting inside for an umbrella to hold over her. From the back seat in the car Becky grinned at Kate. 'The dear man does so enjoy looking after me.'

'Of course he does,' Kate said stoutly, 'and so do I. You've got to behave yourself and not overdo things.'

Becky was installed in a comfortable chair in her sitting-room and Marie bustled in with coffee and a plate of little biscuits, still warm from the oven. She looked as if she was bursting to ply Becky with questions, but, seeing the doctor, she contented herself with welcoming *madame* home and hoping she felt better, before she hurried away.

The doctor had to leave for his local practice almost immediately, only stopping to gulp down a cup of coffee and swallow three biscuits and assure himself that she had all she needed.

'She looks wonderful,' Kate said, as she walked with him to the door. 'I'm sure she knows that she has a lot to thank you for.'

'*Ah, non, non.*' The doctor waved his hands dismissively, but he looked delighted. 'She is a wonderful lady. She is always cheerful and she sees the best in everybody. That is 'alf the battle.'

Cheerful! Yes, that was true of Becky, and it must be true of her, too, for Becky's sake, even though she felt as hard and bitter as an unripe apple.

She found Becky pottering about her sitting-room, lovingly examining what she called her knick-knacks.

'Hey, you're supposed to be resting,' Kate said, stretching her mouth into a smile.

'Oh, but it's so lovely to be back among all my own things. Look, isn't he sweet?' She picked up a little furry rabbit from the mantelpiece. 'A present from a grateful customer. Aren't people nice?' She sighed. 'And anyway, Louis wants me to take exercise; he doesn't believe in sitting about too much after an operation. They let me go early from hospital because he promised to look after me.'

Kate said, 'He's a very nice man, Becky.'

'Yes, he is, isn't he?' Becky stroked the rabbit's ears thoughtfully.

'Is he ... I mean, are you ... ?'

Becky chuckled. 'Louis would like us to be married, but—oh, I don't know. I'm so fond of my little hotel here and he's so busy with his two practices and his hospital work. I think we'll just be good friends for the time being. We'll have to wait and see,' she finished practically. 'Now I want to hear all the news. I feel quite cut off from things here.'

'But not now.' Kate kept her smile intact. 'Marie will be bringing in your lunch soon and then you must rest. This afternoon we can talk and I'll bring you up to date.'

It wasn't going to be easy to explain Will's sudden departure, Kate thought, as she went to the kitchen to help Marie with serving lunch. The plain truth would be easiest—although not quite all of it.

But that afternoon, as she sat in Becky's little sitting-room, pouring out tea, Kate realised that the plain truth made everything more difficult.

'Now tell me about that nice young man I saw in the hospital,' Becky said. 'Will, wasn't it?'

'Will Raven?' Katy spoke his name as casually as she could. 'Oh, he's gone; he left yesterday.'

'Gone? But I thought ...' There was a silence while the keen brown eyes searched Kate's face. 'There's something you're not telling me, isn't there, Katy? I admit my encounter with him in the hospital was quite brief, but he managed to tell me quite a lot in a short time. He explained why you were passing him off as the temporary manager. He also remarked that I wasn't to worry about his being at the hotel alone with you, as he intended to marry you once he'd got you round to the idea. He didn't seem to me like a young man who would give up very easily.' She leaned forward and picked up her teacup. 'So tell me, Katy, love, what happened?'

Kate shrugged. 'What happened was that I found out who he was and why he had come here. I suppose he didn't tell you that he's the son of the woman my father deserted his family for?'

'No!' Becky sank back in her chair again. 'How extraordinary that he should come here!'

'Not really,' Kate said drily. 'My father sent him here to spy. To find out from you how the land lay because he's decided he wants to be friends with me again, now that Mother has gone. Friends!' Kate's voice dripped with contempt. 'After ignoring me for ten years. How despicable can you get? When Will Raven found out that I was here that was a lucky break for him: he was able to worm his way into my—my confidence.' For a moment her voice showed signs of breaking and then she controlled it again. 'Yesterday it all came out and I told him what I thought of him for his part in the lies and the deception. I made it quite clear that I wouldn't see my father again under any circumstances, and that I never wanted to see him again either and I expected him to leave immediately. He left.'

She drew a long breath. 'And that, Becky, dear, is the whole pathetic story, so let's forget all about it, may we?'

She tried to make it non-emotional, as if it had happened to someone else, but she could feel Becky's keen brown eyes searching her face, and she got to her feet quickly. 'I'll go and get some hot water,' she said, picking up the teapot.

'Katy—sit down again.'

Something in Becky's voice made her obey. She sat down and looked at her aunt questioningly.

The small room was suddenly full of tension. The only sound was the rain against the window and the far-off voices of Marie and Jacques in the kitchen.

'Don't make the mistake your mother made.'

'What mistake?'

'The mistake of seeing everything from your own point of view.'

Kate pulled a face, as if she had received a lecture and was taking it good-naturedly. 'Oh, I don't think I do. I always try to——'

But Becky wasn't listening. 'Have you ever wondered, Kate, why your father left your mother?'

Kate stiffened. 'I know why. Mother told me. He left her for a woman who was more sexy than she was. Although she didn't put it quite like that; she put it more—politely.'

'And it *wasn't* quite like that,' Becky said. 'It was rather different.'

There was a longer pause. Kate had a strong urge to get up and walk out, but an even stronger urge to hear what Becky had to say kept her sitting there.

'What do you mean?' Kate was beginning to feel defensive.

'I mean that he left because for over fifteen years she had refused to be a wife to him. After you were born she had a nervous breakdown and she turned against your father. She couldn't bear him near her. I know all this because she told me. I think I was the only person she talked to. I begged her to see a doctor, to go to a psychiatrist. I was a nurse—I knew about these things, and that it sometimes happens like that, and can be put right. But every time I suggested it she flew into a rage and got hysterical. Your father was wonderful with her, very patient and kind. But neither of us could *make* her take advice and there was nothing he could do. In the end he came to accept it. He buried himself in his work, and your mother devoted herself to you. They grew further and further apart. Didn't you ever wonder why they had separate rooms?'

Kate said slowly, 'I don't think I ever thought it was strange; it was just something I grew up with. But——'

Becky lifted a hand. 'Let me go on, dear. After some years of living like that the inevitable happened. Your father met a woman when he was working at his firm's Paris office—a widow with a grown-up son. They fell deeply in love. For your sake he stayed on with your mother and you at home. Then, when you were fifteen, Marguerite—that was the woman's name—became ill with a terminal illness. She was given only a year or two to live. Your father was faced with a terrible choice— your mother didn't need him, but you did, and he loved you dearly. So he had to choose and choose quickly, between leaving you, and leaving the woman he loved to die without the help and love he could give her. The choice nearly broke his heart, I knew that. He guessed what would happen if he left—that your mother would turn you against him—and he couldn't bear to put you through one of those awful tugs of love that you hear about. You were fifteen, he said, nearly grown up and with your first boyfriend. It was better that he should go out of your life. He said he would write to you explaining all that and telling you how much he loved you and always would, and that some day you would come together again. He thought you were mature enough to accept his decision, and he hoped that one day you could come together again. But you never received his letters, did you?'

Kate shook her head unhappily. 'No.'

There was a long silence. Then Kate said, very low, 'I adored him and he left me without a word. I waited and waited, but he never wrote to me. It nearly broke my heart.'

Becky nodded as if she wasn't surprised. 'He *did* write to you, you know. He wrote several times, but when he never got a reply he guessed that his letters had never reached you.'

'You mean . . . Oh, no, Mother would never have . . .'

But she was remembering those early days in the flat. How Mother had always been the first down in the morning, how the post had always been on the breakfast table, how her own longed-for letter had never arrived, and she knew it was true.

'How do you know all this, Becky?' she asked. 'Have you seen him?'

Becky nodded. 'He came to see me the day after he left home. I was working at a hospital in East London. He told me what he was doing and why, and he gave me his address in Paris and begged me to let him know how you were, from time to time, and if you needed anything.'

'*Needed anything*,' Kate said coldly. 'Of course I needed things, and Mother had to work to provide them for me. After the house was sold and the mortgage paid off there was only enough money to buy that horrid little flat. I don't know quite what happened after the divorce, but I know there was never any money except what she earned, not until I was earning myself. I can never forgive him for that.'

Becky shook her head. 'Wrong again, dear, I'm afraid,' she said ruefully.

Kate's smile was very grim. 'Oh, no, Becky, you can't make me believe that. I *know* how poor we were. Mother and I had to scrimp and save to make ends meet. There's no doubt at all about that.'

Becky leaned forward and covered Kate's hand briefly with her own. 'Listen, Katy, I know how rotten you must feel to have to hear all this, but you've got to know the whole truth now.' She paused for a moment, thinking. Then she said, 'Tell me, first, have you heard from your father lately?'

Kate's green eyes were suddenly wary. 'How did you guess? I had a letter from him, via the solicitors. I recognised his handwriting so I tore it up. I didn't read it.'

Becky groaned. 'Oh, dear, then I'll have to tell you myself.'

Kate shook her head wearily. 'More disclosures? I don't think I want to hear anything else.'

Becky said firmly, 'You've got to, my dear. You know half the truth. You've got to know the other half. It's only fair to your father.'

'Fair!' Kate cried. 'When was he ever fair to us?' She got up and walked to the window and stood staring out, her back to Becky.

'Now calm down and come back here,' Becky said. 'There isn't much more to tell you.'

Reluctantly Kate sat down again.

'Well,' Becky began, 'I'll tell it as it happened. About ten days ago—just before I went into hospital, actually—your father suddenly descended on me here. He was in quite a distraught state. He hardly stopped to greet me after all this time. "It's beyond belief," he kept on saying. "I've just found out and I couldn't think of anyone to turn to who might explain it but you." When I'd sat him down and given him a drink he became more lucid. He told me that the money he'd been paying regularly for ten years into your mother's deposit account with her bank had never been used. She'd never drawn out a penny. For ten years it had just been sitting there, gathering interest. "It's a mystery, Becky," he said. "Vera didn't have any money of her own and Kate was all set to go on to college when she left school, and——"'

'It's a lie!' Kate shouted. 'He never gave us any money. Mother always told me he left us without a penny. Or perhaps she never knew about it,' she added more hopefully.

'Oh, she knew all right. Banks send regular statements to their customers, you know. But let me finish. James kept saying, "How the blazes have they managed all this time?" And of course I had to tell him that your mother had worked at a menial job and worn out her health doing it. And that somehow she'd managed to save enough money to help you through college. He was absolutely shattered. He said, "So Kate couldn't have known? My God, Becky, what must she have been thinking of me all these years? I've got to see her to try and put things right." I gave him the address of your flat, but I told him I wasn't sure if you were still there. He said he'd write to you through the solicitors—you'd be sure to get his letter then. I warned him that you might not be very pleased to hear from him and he went off looking absolutely miserable. I've never seen a man more cut up. And that Kate, is all I have to tell you.'

Kate dropped her head into her hands, all her defences gone. At last she lifted her face and said weakly, 'How could Mother have done this? Why?'

Becky said thoughtfully, 'I knew your mother very well, dear. She was always proud and independent. Quick to take offense, slow to forgive. And she was fiercely possessive of you, Katy. I think she wanted you to depend on her for everything. Like all of us she craved for love—your love.'

Kate gave a long sigh. 'Poor Mother—I *did* love her, and I was proud of her. She'd had a very raw deal and she'd coped with it quite heroically.' She shook her head. 'I'm still sorry for her, but for a different reason.'

Becky said, 'You're a very loyal girl, Kate. I can well understand how you feel.'

Kate got to her feet. 'I can't take it all in at once,' she said, turning to the door. 'I've got to get out into the fresh air and think.'

Becky looked through the window, where the rain was still lashing down. 'You'll get soaked, dear...' she began.

But Kate had gone.

She ran out to the garage, not even waiting to put on a coat. She had to get away by herself quickly, quickly. She felt as if little mice were scurrying round in her head, but she pushed them away and got into her Metro. On the main road, she drove as fast as she dared for miles and miles, not allowing herself to think of anything but her driving. At last the click of the windscreen wipers and the sight of the blades waving backwards and forwards before her eyes made her want to scream and she turned off into a narrow side-road, drove a couple of miles along it, and switched off the engine.

The sudden silence wrapped round her like a blanket. The car windows misted over and soon she was sitting isolated from the outside world with only the sound of the rain pattering on the car roof and the distant hum of traffic on the main road.

She sat back and closed her eyes, trying to pull herself together. Her world had turned inside out and upside-down in the space of an hour, but the one thing that filled her mind with black despair was that she'd lost Will. She'd lost him and it was her own fault. 'Don't make the mistake your mother made', Becky had said, and she'd done just that. She'd rejected the man who loved her and he'd turned to another woman.

She with her high moral principles, she thought in bitter self-disgust. She'd been wrong—wrong—wrong. She thumped her fists on the wheel of the car. She'd been wrong about everything. Wrong about Daddy, wrong about Mother, but, worst of all, wrong about Will.

She shivered. With the heater off, the car was getting very cold. She ached to have Will sitting beside her, to turn to him and feel his arm drawing her close against him, to see the teasing smile hovering at the corner of his mouth.

Perhaps, when he read her note, he would phone, would come back. Stop it, you fool, she told herself furiously. Of course he won't come back. What man would want a girl who'd turned out to be a sanctimonious prig? She'd lost him—she'd lost Will, and it was all her own stupid fault. She'd blethered about truth and integrity and hurled dreadful insults at him. She couldn't even remember half of what she'd said.

At that moment she hated herself and all she'd once believed in. And, sitting in the lonely little car in the middle of nowhere, she threw back her head, whimpering like an animal in pain.

CHAPTER ELEVEN

FOR three days Kate never went far from the phone. She still had a faint hope that when Will got her letter he would at least acknowledge it. But, as day followed day and there was no word from him, hope began to fade.

He was never out of her mind for a moment. She read his note over and over again. 'I'm sorry I was such a disappointment to you. I wish you well always'. The words that had touched her heart when she first read them now seemed horribly final.

She knew she ought to go back to London and start making a new life for herself, but she still stayed on, hoping against hope. Something might have happened to her letter—perhaps the posts had been delayed. She couldn't accept that Will would just tear the letter up. Unless he was bitterly angry with her—as angry as she herself had been when she tore Daddy's letter up. Rough justice, she thought bleakly. Oh, it was all such a mess!

Easter was approaching and the hotel was coming back to life. Two girls arrived from the village to do the cleaning. Marie and Jacques made frequent trips to the nearest town to stock up the freezer. Becky was getting back into management, with Pierre's help, and spent some time in the office each day.

Kate fixed a bright smile on her mouth, ignoring the heavy lump that lay in wait for her each morning when she woke up and settled somewhere in her chest, where it stayed all day.

She found little odd jobs for herself in the house and garden, but there was really no need for her to stay on, she knew.

Dr Louis called most evenings, between surgeries, and on Sunday he took Becky for a drive in his car. Kate was invited to join them, but tactfully declined.

The bedroom Kate had been using would be needed for the first lot of visitors, who were due to arrive on Saturday. Kate moved all her things down to Becky's annexe and slept on a put-you-up in the sitting-room. The nights were even more agonising than before now, for she had to make herself lie still and not toss and turn and weep into the pillow as she'd been doing when she was alone upstairs. Her misery was her own stupid fault and she wasn't going to allow Becky to be disturbed.

She couldn't bear much more of this, she decided. She had to act. She just needed to be *sure*. On Wednesday something happened that made her mind up for her. The floppy disk that Will had been using was returned in the post. When Pierre told her of this she hunted through the envelope, but all she could find was Will's card with the words 'Very many thanks' scribbled on it. She sat down in the office chair. This was the end, then, the bitter end.

By the same post a letter arrived for her from Edward. Very formal, very polite, hoping she was enjoying her holiday and requesting her to call at the office as soon as she got back to London, as there were several matters he wished to discuss with her.

The return of the disk and Edward's letter provided Kate with both the spur and the excuse. 'I think I'd better be getting back to London,' she told Becky. 'Things seem to be piling up there. I've got to see about selling the flat and getting a new job and finding somewhere to live. And the solicitors want to see me.'

They were having tea together in Becky's sitting-room. Becky, by now, was looking the picture of health, her greying hair shining again, her brown eyes bright as a squirrel's. 'Well, if you must, you must. But it hasn't been much of a holiday for you—what with one thing and another.'

'Mainly another,' Kate said in an unguarded moment.

Becky looked sharply across the table. 'It's Will Raven, isn't it?'

Kate swallowed and tried to hold on to her smile. 'I don't know what you mean.'

'Oh, yes, you do, dear. I've known you for twenty-five years and it's not difficult to see when you're acting a little white lie.'

If she hadn't said those very words Kate might have kept up the pretence, but suddenly it was all too much and tears flooded into her eyes.

'Hadn't you better tell me about it?' Becky said practically.

Kate bit her lip, nodding. 'I've been an utter fool, that's all.' Then it all came out, the whole story—well, almost the whole story. 'Then, when he'd gone, I wrote a note to him, apologising for what I'd said and asking him to get in touch. That was before you told me about Daddy, but even then I knew I loved Will and I couldn't wait to tell him I'd been wrong, so that night I phoned his flat. And his agent answered the phone. She's been angling for Will—she came here when he was here and made a dead set at him. He said he wasn't interested, but I suppose...' She broke off to wipe her eyes.

'That she's got him on the rebound, as we used to call it?' Becky suggested.

Kate nodded speechlessly.

'And he hasn't replied to your letter?'

'Not a word,' Kate said miserably. 'And I daren't ring up again in case she's still there. I think I'd die.'

Becky thought for a long time and then she said, 'I think you should be brave enough to give it one more try, dear. At least if you speak to him you'll have the satisfaction of knowing the worst.'

'I expect you're right, but I don't know if I can,' Kate said, sniffing. 'I'm not very brave. But in any case, Becky, dear, I think I'll be off tomorrow morning.' She stood up and gave Becky a little hug. 'And thank you for being such an understanding dear,' she said and hurried out of the room. Becky would be embarrassed by a show of gratitude.

For the rest of that day, and while she packed her bags in the evening, she thought over what Becky had said, and by the time she was ready for bed she knew she had to phone Will again.

Once Becky was asleep in bed Kate went out to the phone in the lounge and dialled Will's number. Her stomach was clenched and her hands were numb, but she had to go through with it. She listened to the ringing tone at the other end of the line. It went on and on and she was just about to put down the receiver, almost with relief, when she heard a voice say, 'Hello, who is that?'

Oh, God, Lisbeth! It was true, then. The receiver fell from Kate's hand and dangled on its cord. She groped for it and replaced it. Then she sat dry-eyed in the empty lounge, waiting until she was sure that Becky was asleep before she crawled into her narrow bed.

In the morning Kate was up early. Becky had her breakfast in bed and Kate went in to say goodbye.

'I hate not being up to see you off, Katy,' Becky said. 'But the next time you come it will be a happier time, I promise you.' She asked no questions and Kate didn't mention the thing that must have been in both their minds. But Becky knew.

'Don't worry about me, Becky,' Kate said. 'I'll survive.' She would have to.

Becky said, 'You're a plucky girl, Katy. You always have been. Now take care driving. Which way will you go?'

'I thought I'd take the coast road. It's a bit longer, but I'm not in any hurry and I don't want to go through Rouen.' Too many memories in Rouen.

She kissed Becky goodbye and went out to say goodbye to the others. Jacques carried her bags to the car, and then she was off. Becky was at the window, waving to her, and she waved back cheerfully. A new life, she told herself. You just hang on to that thought, my girl.

The coast road was fairly quiet. Kate drove carefully, drawing in to allow faster cars to pass. She'd been driving for about half an hour when she realised that there was a large grey car driving much too close behind her on a twisty stretch of road. Bother the man! It was bound to be a man—no woman would drive so rudely. Kate was not very kindly disposed towards the male sex just now.

She speeded up and the car behind did likewise. She began to fume. To make matters worse, the sun was shining straight into her eyes. As soon as she got to a straight stretch of road she slowed down. 'OK, come on, you brute,' she muttered aloud.

The grey car shot past her—and immediately slowed down again. So he wanted to play silly games, did he? OK, she'd call his bluff. She drew on to the grass verge and stopped.

Horrors! The car in front was stopping too. She went icy cold. She knew what could happen to solitary women drivers on lonely roads. She could see the banner head-lines waving in front of her eyes. With a terrible fasci-nation she stared at the rear bumper of the grey car as it backed slowly towards the Metro until it was only a couple of feet away. The sun was dazzling her, but she was conscious of the door of the car in front swinging open and a man jumping out.

She thought quickly. If she put the Metro into reverse she could swing round and get back on the road. Then, with a head start, she might find a farmhouse that would give her refuge. She pushed out the clutch and took off the handbrake. Her palm was slippery with sweat as she struggled for the knob of the gear lever. Out of the corner of her eye she saw a dark form looming up at the side window as she managed to get into gear. She let in the clutch too quickly, the car jumped backwards, the engine stalled, and the car stopped dead.

The man was banging on the window now, shouting something and rattling the door-handle. Thank heaven the door was locked. She always locked the driving door when she was alone, as a precaution against just such a hideous emergency as this.

She fumbled for the ignition key, but the gear was still in reverse, and another jump backwards was the only result.

The man was leaning down to the window now. Kate took in a long breath and forced herself to look round. She stared glassily at the face framed in the window.

'Come on, Kate,' shouted Will. 'Open this damned door.'

She thought she was going to faint. She slumped back in her seat, but her hand went out and pushed up the door lock. It opened.

Will's head was on a level with hers as he peered in. 'What's the matter? Are you all right?'

'No,' she croaked. 'I'm not all right. You scared the wits out of me.'

'Oh, did I?' With no greeting or apology he went on. 'I had to stop you somehow or we should have been in the English Channel. I got your letter this morning and I've come to find out what it's all about.'

Kate's tongue touched her dry lips. 'How did you know...?'

'I've seen Becky. She told me you were coming this way.' He glanced round at his powerful car. 'I reckoned I might just about catch up with you.' He smiled, but it wasn't a pleasant smile. Will was very, very angry.

Well, she wasn't amused herself. 'Catch up with me? You nearly drove me off the road.'

She craned her neck to look up at him, and in the sunlight she saw that he looked desperately tired. His face was pale, his eyes were faintly bloodshot and there were dark shadows beneath them. Will had been living it up. 'Are we going to stay here all day?' she said.

'Certainly not. Come on, get out.'

'I don't see why——' she began.

'Out, I said!'

Something in his voice frightened her. 'You're drunk,' she said. But she thought it best to obey. She got out of the car and stood beside him.

'Now lock the door,' he ordered. 'We won't need your car again just yet.'

She took the key out of the lock automatically and as she hesitated he grabbed it and locked the door.

'We can't just leave the car here,' she wailed. 'It might be stolen, or anything. And my luggage is in the boot.'

Bill unlocked the boot, heaved out her two heavy bags, and tossed them on to the rear seat of his own car. Then he took her by the arm and pushed her none too gently into the passenger-seat.

'What is this?' Kate demanded. 'A kidnap?'

Will put the car into gear and it moved smoothly away, gathering speed by the second. 'You could call it that,' he said. 'I'm certainly holding on to you until I get some satisfaction.'

Kate looked back over her shoulder as the big grey car streaked ahead. Her fast-receding Metro looked forlorn, standing all alone beside the deserted road. She felt confused and nervous, but Will was with her again. He was very angry but he was here, sitting beside her, and to Kate that was the most important thing in the world.

She looked up sideways at him as the car began to eat up the kilometres at an alarming rate. He was looking straight ahead. His mouth was set in a hard line, his hair slightly unkempt. Perhaps it was a reflection from the yellow sweater he was wearing, but his cheeks seemed to have an unhealthy pallor. He was quite obviously seething with anger held under control. She'd never seen him like this, even when they parted in the lane. She began to tremble. Somehow she must get through to him. 'You're driving again. Is your leg quite better, then?'

'Yes, thanks,' he replied curtly.

There was a long silence. Then Kate tried again. 'Where are we going?' she asked.

'Paris,' he snapped. She gave it up and that was the last word that either of them spoke until, at last, the car pulled up in the forecourt of an enormous block of luxury apartments in what Kate supposed to be Paris. She had never been to Paris and was in no mood to enjoy the scenery.

She was rigid with tension. Will must have broken every traffic regulation on the journey.

He gripped her arm as she got out of the car and led her, as if he were a gaoler, into a lift to the top floor and into an expensively furnished penthouse apartment.

Kate felt exhausted. She looked unseeingly round the long room and through the wide windows at the city spread out below. 'Sit down,' Will barked, and pushed her into the corner of a deep velvet sofa. She had no energy to resist his bullying tactics.

He stood over her, scowling down. 'Now,' he said, 'I want some explanations.'

She controlled her quivering lips. 'I won't say a word while you stand there like a—a counsel for the prosecution.'

He drew up a small chair and sat down facing her, staring fixedly into her huge troubled green eyes.

'I want a few things clear,' he said. 'I want to know why you've put me through it. After what we had together that last night...then the next morning you turn

on me and accuse me of all manner of dreadful things
and order me off the premises. I don't consider that anything I did could merit that treatment. It hurt like hell,
Kate.'

Her head jerked back. 'It didn't take you very long
to console yourself,' she said.

'What are you talking about?' he demanded roughly.

Kate drew in a short breath and her throat ached.
'Almost as soon as you'd gone I knew I'd been wrong.
I wrote to you and posted the letter. But I couldn't wait
until it reached you. Later that night I telephoned your
flat here, and Lisbeth answered. I recognised her voice
immediately, and I heard you speaking to her. She said...'
Her voice choked up. 'She said, "Hurry, Willy-boy! I'm
waiting." And I hung up the receiver.'

Bill uttered a couple of words in French that Kate
could only guess at. 'And you really believed that I'd
gone to bed with Lisbeth, straight out of your bed the
night before? You thought that of me?'

'What else could I think?' Kate said in a small voice.
'It was one o'clock in the morning.'

He groaned. 'Yes,' he said heavily. 'I see. Well, I won't
trot out the old cliché, "It's not what you think", but
I'll tell you exactly what happened that day. And,' he
added fiercely, 'you'd better believe me, because it's the
truth.'

'I'll believe you.' Kate sank back into the vast recesses
of the sofa. Of course she'd believe him. There weren't
going to be any more lies between them now.

Will pushed back his chair and sat on the sofa beside
her, but not touching her, locked his hands between his
knees, and looked down at the carpets, as if remembering every detail. He said at last, 'When I got to Paris
I couldn't face an empty flat. Jimbo—your father—
wasn't due home until the following week. First of all I
went to my computer people and told them to copy the

disk I'd borrowed and return it to you. I left my card
and the address of the hotel.'

So that was why there had been no letter with the disk!
She drew in a breath and he glanced up at her
questioningly.

'Go on,' she said.

'After that I went to a cinema and sat through the
programme without seeing a thing. Then I just walked
about the streets for hours, trying to think what I'd done
to deserve all the flak you'd thrown at me, and I was
torn between anger and resentment and utter black
misery at losing you. Eventually I found myself in the
restaurant I usually frequent. I ate a little and drank a
good deal. It got late and I was bracing myself to go
home to bed, and not looking forward to it, when who
should appear but Lisbeth, all bright-eyed and bushy-
tailed, as usual. She was with a party, but she latched
on to me. She was on the way to a book fair in Monte
Carlo, she explained. My publishers had a stand and were
displaying my new book. She thought it would boost
sales if I put in a personal appearance, and would I drive
to Monte with her. I was beyond caring what I did and
I thought, What the hell, why not? So I took her back
to the apartment to wait while I changed and tried to
regain some sort of sanity. Then we drove down through
the night.' He glared at Kate. 'I said we *drove* through
the night. Do you believe me?'

She gave him a little smile. 'I believe you.'

'Well, that's a nice change,' Will said wryly. 'To con-
tinue... In Monte, Lisbeth made a hit with a rich
American film producer and decided to go back to Paris
with him a couple of days later. But I stayed around,
meeting up with old cronies, losing quite a lot of money
at the tables, and drinking far too much—all the well-
known remedies for a broken heart. By yesterday
morning I was sick of the whole silly show and my heart
hadn't recovered in the slightest degree, so I got on a

train to Paris. When I opened the door of the flat there
was a message from Lisbeth on the answerphone. She'd
landed me a plum contract with her film producer and
could she come round and get me to sign it? I agreed.
She came. She stayed about half an hour and then went
back to her American. This morning I went through the
piles of letters, found yours, and drove straight down to
the hotel. The rest you know.'

He got to his feet and paced restlessly about the room.
Then he came back and stood in front of Kate. 'And
now,' he said, 'hadn't you better tell me your side of the
story?'

She patted the sofa. 'Sit down beside me. I can't talk
while you're prowling about like a tiger.'

'I feel like a tiger,' he said, and sat down at the opposite corner of the sofa, not touching her.

Kate stared down at her hands. 'Not very much to
tell,' she said. 'I'm not very proud of myself. I've been
really neurotic about my father for years. I adored him,
trusted him, and when he left without a word I thought
he'd rejected me. That hurt much more than when my
mother told me he'd left us penniless. That's what I believed—until Becky told me the whole truth. That belief
has eaten further and further into me through the years.
That's why I could never speak about him, or even think
about him. I persuaded myself that I hated him. And
when I heard that you were close to him, that he'd sent
you to find out about me...well, I just went over the
top. Something snapped. I'm sorry, Will, it was unfair.'

He was looking hard at her, a little frown creasing his
forehead. He said, 'When did you say you found out
the truth from Becky?'

'Oh, about a week ago.'

'And yet you wrote that letter to me as soon as I'd
left, before you knew you'd been wrong about Jimbo,
that he'd loved you all the time—the truth that you
wouldn't hear from me. Why, Kate?'

She smiled. 'Now I understand why you write mysteries. You never miss a clue, do you?'

He moved further along the sofa towards her. 'Come on,' he said, inching nearer. 'Tell me.'

Kate looked into his face. His eyes were brilliant, his mouth twisting with tenderness.

Her heart shook. 'Because I love you,' she said softly.

His arms drew her close. 'Oh, my sweet Kate,' he groaned. 'I've been in hell this last week.'

'I've been there too,' she said shakily. 'What a pity we didn't meet. We could have saved a lot of time.'

He stood up and pulled her to her feet. 'Don't let's waste any more,' he said. 'My bed's big enough for two. Yes?'

She wound her arms round his neck and rubbed her cheek against his. 'Oh, yes,' she murmured.

Then they both froze as they heard the front door open. A man's voice called, 'Hello—anyone at home? Will?'

'Jimbo!' breathed Will, and, frantically, 'Darling, I didn't know. This isn't a trick, I swear it.'

He crossed to the door in three quick strides and opened it, standing in the opening so that Kate's view into the hall was blocked.

But the man's voice reached her clearly. 'Oh, lord, Will, I'm whacked. The contract went through in record time for once and I found myself with three days to spare. I didn't fancy hanging round Tokyo so I got on the first flight and came home.'

Kate felt nothing except the cold numbness of shock. Her eyes were fixed on the door and when it opened further and her father walked into the room she still felt nothing.

He stopped dead, with a harsh intake of breath. 'My God, Kathy!'

Her mind registered that he had changed a lot. He wasn't as tall as she remembered and his hair was quite grey.

Her eyes moved to Will and he shrugged slightly in helpless apology. The three of them were standing quite still, Kate facing the two men across the room. How extraordinary, she thought; we're like actors in a play. They're waiting for me to speak my next line and I don't know what it is. She must think of something to say to break the horrible silence, but nothing came.

Her eyes fixed themselves on her father's face. She saw the deep furrows across his brow, and his blue eyes that had once been so vivid now looked dull. His mouth drooped at the corners. He looked—defeated.

Suddenly Kate thought, He's old.

There was a lump in her throat and her inside squeezed up with pity and love.

She knew what her line was. She gave him a crooked smile. 'Hello, Jimbo,' she said. And in her use of the little pet name lay her acceptance of what had gone before and all her hopes for the future.

She saw the tension drain out of his face. He came towards her and his arms went out to her tentatively.

She ran towards him and was held tightly against him, her face buried in his shirt. Impulsively she reached out to Will to draw him into the circle, and all three were locked together.

Kate gulped, 'I th-think I'm going to cry,' and already tears were streaming down her cheeks.

'Me, too,' muttered James gruffly.

Will thrust a large handkerchief towards Kate. 'I always did like a good weepie,' he remarked.

Kate blew her nose and wiped her eyes. Trust Will to lower the emotional temperature. She began to giggle.

And then they were all three laughing together. James had collapsed into a chair and the other two on to the sofa.

James couldn't take his eyes off his daughter. 'She's beautiful,' he kept on saying. 'She's so beautiful. Isn't she beautiful, Will?' as if she were some priceless object he'd just found.

Will looked smug. 'The first moment I saw her I thought she was the most beautiful girl I'd ever seen. And the second moment I decided I had to have her for myself.'

'That's a lie,' Kate broke in indignantly. 'You were absolutely horrid to me.'

'Oh, give or take half an hour,' he said, contentedly squeezing her waist. 'Which brings us to the next point.' He stood up and stood stiffly to attention before James. 'May I have your permission, sir, to marry your daughter?' he said with mock formality. 'I believe the lady is willing.'

James lay back in his chair. 'Well, I'm damned! No sooner do I acquire a daughter than some fellow wants to take her away from me.'

He stood up, smiling delightedly at them both, kissing Kate, shaking hands with Will. 'This calls for champagne. Have we got any, Will?'

'You bet we have,' Will said and disappeared into the kitchen.

Alone with Kate, James perched on the edge of the sofa beside her, gripping her hand hard. 'Is it all right, Kathy, have you forgiven me? Is it really all right? I can hardly believe it.'

She nodded, her eyes shining. 'It's really all right. It's wonderful.'

Will returned with the champagne and glasses, and after the toasts and congratulations they all decided they were hungry, but didn't want to go out to a restaurant. So they settled for Will's special Welsh rarebit and sat round the kitchen table to eat it. They laughed a lot, talked about nothing in particular, and Kate thought dreamily that she'd never been as happy as this in all her life.

At last James stood up, yawning. 'Well, I'm for bed if I'm going to avoid jet lag. Goodnight, Kathy, darling.' He bent and kissed her. 'Goodnight, Will. Bless you, my children.'

At the door he turned. 'I expect the two of you will make your own sleeping arrangements,' he said blandly, and he went out and closed the door.

Will slid a glance towards Kate. 'There's tact for you.'

Suddenly Kate felt shy. She piled up the dishes, carried them across to the sink, and turned the tap on with a gush. Coming up behind her, Will reached round and turned it off again.

'This has been a pretty big thing for you, hasn't it?' he said quietly, and she nodded speechlessly, her head bent.

'I think I can understand.' He put an arm round her shoulder and she shivered.

His voice was very low, close to her ear. 'Come to bed, my dearest,' he said.

He made love to her slowly, intensely, and when it was over Kate lay beside him relaxed, utterly fulfilled. She put her lips against the smooth tip of his shoulder. 'Oh, that was wonderful,' she sighed.

He propped himself up, gazing down at her. 'You're wonderful,' he said in a voice that sent little thrills up and down her spine. 'I love everything about you to utter distraction, my Kate. I love your hair.' He stroked the silky dark red tresses that were spread out on the pillow. 'And your eyes—I could swim in those gorgeous green eyes—and your smile.' Then his eyes travelled down the length of her white body. 'You're perfect,' he breathed.

'But there's something more than lust,' he went on. 'I love your honesty, your integrity, your generosity, the way you can admit that you've been wrong. Oh, so many things—I haven't got the right words.' He trailed off into a string of French.

Kate sighed. 'I wish I knew French. Will you teach me?'

'Of course. You can have your first lesson now. Repeat after me "*Je t'adore*".'

Kate's green eyes sparkled up at him. 'I can guess that one. *Je t'adore, mon cher Will*.' She mimicked his accent.

He laughed with delight and kissed her. 'Ten out of ten. We'll have the next lesson tomorrow. But now, perhaps you should sleep—you must be tired. *Are* you tired?' he added hopefully.

'Desperately.' She smiled a secret smile, snuggling down under the duvet. She laid her arm across his smooth, flat stomach and eased herself closer to him. 'But not so tired that you couldn't wake me up if you tried very hard. Will you, Will?'

She didn't have to wait for his answer.

EPILOGUE

THREE months later, when all the summer flowers were in bloom, Mr and Mrs Will Raven walked hand in hand along a quiet, sandy path in the Monet garden in Giverny.

'Wonderful! Magical!' Kate drew in a deep breath of the warm, scented air. 'You never told me it was like this.'

'My powers of description fall very short when it comes to describing this place,' Will admitted. He stopped looking around. 'God! To think that one man planned all this!'

Kate's eyes followed his and she could sense the emotion he felt for the place. 'My mother brought me here when I was about ten,' he said. 'It was her favourite place. She did some painting herself, but after she'd visited Giverny she always went home and tore her efforts up.' His eyes were tender, remembering. 'I thought they were rather good.'

They strolled on slowly. Everywhere they looked great banks of colour glowed and glistened in the sunlight. Masses of gentian blue merged with azure. Tiny white bell-like flowers peeped out between fronds of deep purple clematis. Shell-pink drifted into rose, into misty heliotrope. Further along, intense summer colours blazed in dramatic schemes—masses of scarlet poppies and nasturtiums of every hue tumbled and rioted against a background of green. The air was full of the drone of bees. Butterflies settled, drank their fill, and then fluttered on to the next source of supply.

Kate and Will strolled on, regardless of other people, alone in their own world. Presently they drew aside to

182

allow a party of ladies to pass, chattering, pointing out, exclaiming. When they had gone Kate said, 'Did you hear one of them say it's like fairyland? And it is, isn't it? You expect to see Oberon and Titania coming through the leaves to meet you.' She smiled reminiscently. 'I played Queen Titania once, when the school put on *A Midsummer Night's Dream*. I had a lovely silver crown.' She peeped up at Will through her lashes. 'And I was bewitched and fell in love with an ass with lovely long silky ears.'

'I hope you're not making insinuations,' said Will, fingering his ears.

'Of *course* not!' Kate said piously. She thought for a moment. 'But I must have been bewitched. There was I, a young woman of twenty-five, with good business qualifications, considering marriage to a steady, reliable, sober citizen, upwardly mobile——'

'Don't remind me.' Will shuddered.

'And then a charming, quite unreliable character appeared, and I was bewitched.'

'And you fell in love with the ass,' Will chuckled, and kissed her. 'Any regrets?'

'Not a single one.' She linked her arm with his and cuddled close.

Soon they arrived at a long, two-storey house with green shutters at the windows. The beds in front were filled with roses tumbling over pink geraniums. 'This was where Monet lived,' Will said. 'It's a museum now. It's fascinating, but I think we'll give it a miss today and come back out of season when it's less crowded. I want to show you the water garden. You have to go through a tunnel under the road to reach it.'

They walked to the entrance. 'Isn't it strange?' Will mused. 'I planned to bring you here on our honeymoon, but as it turns out we're visiting it on someone else's honeymoon.'

'It was a lovely wedding,' Kate said. 'Becky and Louis both looked so happy. Becky always said she'd never give up her beloved hotel, but she won't really have to. Pierre has turned out such a treasure and she can leave a lot to him. I'm sure they'll make a go of it.'

At the entrance to the tunnel they met a party of schoolchildren coming the other way. 'Good,' said Will as they descended the steps. 'We might even have the water garden to ourselves.'

The tunnel was cool and smelled of damp leaves. Before they were halfway through the lights went out and they were plunged into darkness.

'Oh!' Kate gave a little squeal. 'What's happened?'

'Silly me—I'd forgotten there was a time-switch at the entrance.' Will sounded innocent.

'Very convenient, I must say, but I don't believe a word of it,' Kate murmured against his lips. 'And by the way,' she added, disentangling herself from his arms, 'the other day I heard all about your biggest white lie of the lot.'

'Oh?' he asked uneasily.

'Yes, I was talking to Jimbo and mentioned that story of yours about falling off the dressing-table trying to catch a spider. The truth wouldn't be that you risked your life rescuing a small boy from under a car, would it?'

There was a long pause. Then Will said, 'Jimbo will have to answer for this. Would you rather have a hero for a husband than a clown—or an ass?'

'I'll settle for what I've got,' Kate told him, winding her arms round his neck in the darkness. 'Oh, darling, darling, Will, I do love you so terribly.'

When at last they emerged from the tunnel Will's hopes were almost realised. There were only a few visitors here, mostly gathered on the Japanese bridge which spanned the pond at the narrower end.

The contrast with the dazzling beauty of the colour garden was complete. Here the air was cool and the dense green of the tall trees that formed a perfect background for the stretch of still water almost blotted out the sunlight. On the pool, great lily-pads threw up their flat, pinkish-white flowers and wistaria hung mauve tresses from the bridge down to the water.

Kate and Will strolled along the path under the willows, relishing the cool beauty of the place and talking about the delightful subject of their future together.

'You won't mind living in France?' Will asked. 'Because if you'd rather go back to London——'

'I love living in France,' Kate said firmly. 'There's so much to find out about Paris, and I adore shopping in the markets, and I can almost always make myself understood now,' she added proudly.

'And you don't yearn after having a job?'

'I've got a job, haven't I? Being your secretary is almost a full-time job. They say all writers need a good wife.' She grinned. 'Besides, it's going to be exciting fitting up our cottage. I've enjoyed living in the apartment and getting to know Jimbo again after all these years, but it'll be marvellous to have a place all of our own in the country and we can always go back to Paris when we feel like it.' She tucked her arm cosily through his and laid her head against his shoulder. 'Aren't we lucky?'

The water garden was deserted now except for themselves. They climbed up on to the Japanese bridge and stood leaning over the parapet, gazing down into the still water.

'You could stand here for hours,' Kate said, and she spoke very softly, almost as if they were in a great cathedral. 'Look at the way the trees reflect, shading from gold to darkest green. And the patches of blue sky, and the way the wistaria looks deep purple.'

She leaned further over. 'You can see the reflections going down and down, if you look. First bluey, then grey, and right at the bottom almost black. Monet must have spent weeks here, painting his marvellous pictures of the pond.'

She turned to Will, her eyes shining, but he wasn't looking at the water; he was looking at her. 'There's one reflection in the water that Monet didn't see,' he said mysteriously.

She leaned further over, peering deep into the water. 'What reflection? I can't see anything else.'

Will put his arm around her shoulders, his other hand pointing down to the glassy surface of the pond. 'The reflection of the most beautiful flower in the whole garden. Yours, my love,' said Will.

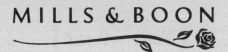

MILLS & BOON

EXCITING NEW COVERS

To reflect the ever-changing contemporary romance series we've designed new covers which perfectly capture the warmth, glamour and sophistication of modern-day romantic situations.

We know, because we've designed them with your comments in mind, that you'll just love the bright, warm, romantic colours and the up-to-date new look.

WATCH OUT FOR THESE NEW COVERS

From October 1993   Price £1.80

Available from W.H. Smith, John Menzies, Martins, Forbuoys, most supermarkets and other paperback stockists. Also available from Mills & Boon Reader Service, Freepost, PO Box 236, Thornton Road, Croydon, Surrey CR9 9EL. (UK Postage & Packing free)

Proudly present
to you...

BETTY NEELS' 100TH ROMANCE

Betty has been writing for Mills & Boon Romances for over 20 years. She began once she had retired from her job as a Ward Sister. She is married to a Dutchman and spent many years in Holland. Both her experiences as a nurse and her knowledge and love of Holland feature in many of her novels.

Her latest romance *'AT ODDS WITH LOVE'* is available from August 1993, price £1.80.

Accept 4 FREE Romances and 2 FREE gifts

FROM READER SERVICE

Here's an irresistible invitation from Mills & Boon. Please accept our offer of 4 FREE Romances, a CUDDLY TEDDY and a special MYSTERY GIFT! Then, if you choose, go on to enjoy 6 captivating Romances every month for just £1.80 each, postage and packing FREE. Plus our FREE Newsletter with author news, competitions and much more.

Send the coupon below to: Mills & Boon Reader Service, FREEPOST, PO Box 236, Croydon, Surrey CR9 9EL.

NO STAMP REQUIRED

Yes! Please rush me 4 FREE Romances and 2 FREE gifts! Please also reserve me a Reader Service subscription. If I decide to subscribe I can look forward to receiving 6 brand new Romances for just £10.80 each month, post and packing FREE. If I decide not to subscribe I shall write to you within 10 days - I can keep the free books and gifts whatever I choose. I may cancel or suspend my subscription at any time. I am over 18 years of age.

Ms/Mrs/Miss/Mr _____ EP55R

Address _____

_____

Postcode _____ Signature _____

MAILING PREFERENCE SERVICE

EXPERIENCE THE EXOTIC

VISIT . . . INDONESIA, TUNISIA, EGYPT AND MEXICO . . . THIS SUMMER

Enjoy the experience of exotic countries
with our Holiday Romance Pack

Four exciting new romances by favourite
Mills & Boon authors.

Available from July 1993   Price: £7.20

Next Month's Romances

Each month you can choose from a wide variety of romance with Mills & Boon. Below are the new titles to look out for next month, why not ask either Mills & Boon Reader Service or your Newsagent to reserve you a copy of the titles you want to buy – just tick the titles you would like and either post to Reader Service or take it to any Newsagent and ask them to order your books.

Please save me the following titles:	Please tick	√
SIMPLY IRRESISTIBLE	Miranda Lee	
HUNTER'S MOON	Carole Mortimer	
AT ODDS WITH LOVE	Betty Neels	
A DANGEROUS MAGIC	Patricia Wilson	
TOWER OF SHADOWS	Sara Craven	
THE UNMARRIED BRIDE	Emma Goldrick	
SWEET BETRAYAL	Helen Brooks	
COUNTERFEIT LOVE	Stephanie Howard	
A TEMPORARY AFFAIR	Kate Proctor	
SHADES OF SIN	Sara Wood	
RUTHLESS STRANGER	Margaret Mayo	
BITTERSWEET LOVE	Cathy Williams	
CAPTIVE BRIDE	Rosemary Carter	
WILLING OR NOT	Liza Hadley	
MASTER OF NAMANGILLA	Mons Daveson	
LOVE YOUR ENEMY	Ellen James	
A FOOLISH HEART	Laura Martin	

If you would like to order these books in addition to your regular subscription from Mills & Boon Reader Service please send £1.80 per title to: Mills & Boon Reader Service, Freepost, P.O. Box 236, Croydon, Surrey, CR9 9EL, quote your Subscriber No:.................................... (If applicable) and complete the name and address details below. Alternatively, these books are available from many local Newsagents including W.H.Smith, J.Menzies, Martins and other paperback stockists from 13 August 1993.

Name:...

Address:...

....Post Code:............................

To Retailer: If you would like to stock M&B books please contact your regular book/magazine wholesaler for details.

You may be mailed with offers from other reputable companies as a result of this application. If you would rather not take advantage of these opportunities please tick box ☐